Cobble Creek

Stories and Poetry

Bob Weir

Illustrations by Marlene Weir

Press On Publishing
Press-On-Publishing.com
RobertMWeir.com
Robert@RobertMWeir.com

Written by Robert M. Weir © 2002
Illustrated by Marlene Weir © 2002
Front Cover Photo by Robert M. Weir © 2002
Back Cover Photo by Marlene Weir © 2002
All Rights Reserved

Designed by Kimberly S. Graham
Printed by Fidlar Doubleday, Inc. on recycled paper

Printed in the United States of America
ISBN 0-9717491-0-8

To
Marge Weir, my mom
Martin Weir, my dad
John Sullivan, artist and inspiration

*Nothing in the world can take
the place of persistence.*

*Talent will not; nothing is more common
than unsuccessful people with talent.*

*Genius will not; unrewarded genius
is almost a proverb.*

*Education will not; the world
is full of educated derelicts.*

*Persistence and determination
alone are omnipotent.*

Press on.

— Author unknown

Contents

Cobble Creek	3
Sentry	4
Determination	7
Porkies	10
What You Didn't Say	14
Cades Cove	17
Cosby Shelter	18
Pathways	20
The Fence	24
The First Train	35
The Third Train	36
John	38
Give From Her	42
Room to Play	52
Doll Room	54
Kreager and Phelps	57
Vegetable Beef Soup	65
Thanksgiving at the Parisville Bar	72
Black of the Moonless Night	79
Full Moon Gathering	81
Unexpected	84
Age 12	85
The First Thing I'm Gonna Do	89
Oh, Gluttonous Christmas Tree	90
Strawberries *(an essay)*	92
Author Biography	95

Cobble Creek

*Today, I walked knee-deep in a cobble creek
moving slowly on unseen stones to keep
from hurting my tender feet.*

*And learned my calm to keep
for my aging dad and
his slow, cautious feet.*

Sentry

The milk bottle was on duty at the cemetery. It stood half full of darkening water next to a pipe that protruded from fresh-mown grass. The old man walked toward it; his feet, clad in thick-soled, slate-gray shoes, skimmed just far enough above the ground to avoid stumbling. He bent from the waist, his rounded shoulders covered by two jackets as a chill October breeze blew from overcast skies, rattled large oak trees, and carried rusty leaves on a diagonal slant toward the earth. The man raised the bottle to the spigot and turned the handle. As the bottle filled, he tensed his arms so the additional weight caused him to stoop only a little more. He then shuffled back to the grave where he had stood a few moments before, to where his wife lay beneath a layer of sod that had been disturbed, then replaced, exactly one year earlier.

They had been wed for 16 years, marrying later in life, when their sense of adventure was soon to be replaced with stiffness and sitting. Yet she found shelter in her rosary, confirming each day her belief in Our Father, Mary who was full of grace and blessed among women, and her own role as a sinner until her muscles nerved up and tightened into rigid steel and a chunk of rust broke loose and ruptured her heart. Afterwards, the man, who now signed himself with the cross, complained about 911: They save all the people on TV; why didn't they save her? And in the year that followed, he stopped watching heroic rescue shows and, instead, took up her holy pilgrimage, adding an extra rosary to his daily prayer.

During that year, as he watched "Jeopardy," "Wheel of Fortune," and other shows that she liked, he would hear her comment and turn in his chair and speak to her. He held doors for her and imagined she was still beside him in the car.

He felt her body, clad in head-to-toe nightgown, snuggle close to his back as he lay on his side in bed at night. He knew she was listening to his prayers, beseeching his eternal salvation, as certainly as hers was already attained.

He watered the potted geranium first, then dusty millers and daisies and mint planted in the ground. His face was somber, his lower lip and chin sagging from his cheeks; yet, from deep within, duty stirred: If you have a garden, what part would you not water? And so he shuffled back to the spigot and refilled the bottle, returning, emptying, and refilling it again six times until all the flowers, including another geranium in an urn on a nearby grave, had been properly benefacted.

Then he returned to the pipe that marked the bottle's resting place and filled it one more time, to the brim, and left it, on duty, for the next time or the next gravetender in the next season.

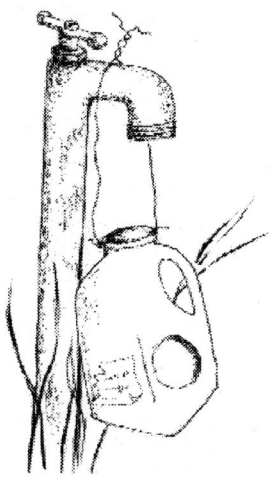

Marge (Schulte) Weir with Martin Weir, Alfredo Careaga, Robert Weir, Emma Schulte and Theresa Weir

Determination

I was barely a freshman at Port Huron Junior College, sitting in English 101, on September 15, 1966, when someone came to the room with a message for me. I knew what the message said.

My mom had had cancer for four years. Four years. That was my high school career. A freshman when I learned of the disease and a freshman again when she died.

Liver cancer. Not one of the fast ones that takes a person in a few months or a year, but one of the slow ones that drags on and on. But, then, she also made it drag on. My mom was determined to see me graduate.

She must have weighed 140 when I was a freshman in high school, but only 90-something when my dad pushed her into the gymnasium in a wheel chair. She wore one of her favorite summery print dresses. We took a picture of the whole family: Mom and Dad, my two grandmothers, myself, and Alfredo Careaga, our foreign exchange student from Bolivia who could play piano like no one I had ever met. Alfredo spent a lot of time at our house our senior year, talking and laughing and banging out great rock 'n' roll on an old beat-up nearly-in-tune upright while Mom lay in her bed upstairs.

We spent a lot of time with Mom — Alfredo and me. But, then, many people spent a lot of time with her.

Mary McCabe was a nurse, retired. In the last months, Mary came by daily or several times a day with a shot. A pain killer that Mom accepted but didn't like. She would have rather kept going on her own. Mary would always stay to talk and talk and talk.

Oh, there was Phyllis Morgan and Mary Jo Dunn and Jo Collins and other ladies from the Daughters of Isabella. When Mom could get up, they played cards, for her friends also belonged to the "Daughters of the Deck" and the "Daughters of the Bingo."

Mom had done so much for so many people. President of the D. of I., involved with the school and the V.F.W., sometimes in charge of the St. Patrick's Day Banquet. Yeah, here was a Weir (nee Schulte), a French/German from a farm in Harbor Beach, working along with pure-blooded Emmett Irishmen like the Culhanes, Keegans, Mullallys, Graces, and Keoghs. She always fit in.

She would disagree, but she was sainthood material. Catholic all her life. Went to church every Sunday that she could. In her last months, the priest came to her. Sometimes on Sunday mornings, Mary McCabe would bring her needle, and Fr. Farrell would bring the Blessed Sacrament. One for the body, and one for the soul.

I don't remember how I knew that attending my graduation was important to her. There was no one statement or event that told me that. I guess I just always knew. Maybe I took it for granted that she would be there. Maybe that was my early unconscious credit to her determination. I just knew. Maybe it was because we had done some wonderful things together while I was in high school, especially after I got my driver's license.

She had a favorite seamstress in Marysville. As Mom lost weight, we visited her often. Take in a seam here, a tuck there. Make it look like it's supposed to be. One summer day — I must have been 16 — after visiting the seamstress, Mom said, "Let's do something special." She told me to drive south out of Marysville toward St. Clair. We took the scenic road next to the blue river and under blue skies. Gorgeous day. All that was pretty special to me because it was an extra distance, Mom and I were together on one of her better days, and, most importantly, I was driving. Yeah, let's go some miles here, Ma.

We stopped at the St. Clair Inn. At first, this did not mean much to me. Sure, it was a beautiful place, right next to the St. Clair River, with lots of windows so we could see Ontario on the other side. The surprise came during the meal when Mom said, "Don't tell your dad we came here. We can't afford this." Then I knew it was special to her, too, because I had never dreamt that my mom would keep anything from my dad. Well, Mom, I've never told him, but I think I will soon. He'll understand. We might talk about how long you must have saved for that luncheon for two at the St. Clair Inn.

Maybe I knew Mom would be at graduation because she had simply made plans to be there. After all, she had made plans for her funeral. She had contacted the funeral director, viewed caskets, and made two selections: mauve if she died in the fall or winter, blue if she died in the spring or summer. Then she picked her best two dresses, one that matched each casket. It seems that she had those two altered more than any other dress, always ready, just in case.

But she wasn't ready to die until I graduated. Yes, she was there. Print dress, pillbox hat, gaunt face, and a weak smile. And a wheelchair. She would have pushed herself to that school if she had to.

Then, three months later, she was gone. In body, that is. In soul, never.

I think she's the reason I've kept a statement I found about a decade ago and strive to live by today. It reads:

"Nothing in the world can take the place of persistence. Talent will not; nothing is more common than unsuccessful people with talent. Genius will not; unrewarded genius is almost a proverb. Education will not; the world is full of educated derelicts. Persistence and determination alone are omnipotent. Press on."

Thank you, Mom. I love you.

Porkies

"You have porkies in the United States, don't you?" Gerald asked me, drawing out his vowels — "poooorkieees" — as much as he clipped his consonants. We were sitting in the Life Boat Inn — "A Family Beer Garden, Dogs Allowed" — near the beach on South Hayling Island. A black Lab curled under a pub stool next to the bar. "You know, white lies or April Fools? You have those in the States, don't you?"

I nodded, wondering where Gerald was leading me. My last full day in England, the day after finishing my business there, had been leisurely. I had slept, read, and waded on the beach. As afternoon waned, I had explored clustered rows of colorful beach huts — about 10 feet by 10 feet in which people store beach chairs and other paraphernalia — and came upon a bright yellow and white cement-block building with a sign that promoted "hot sugared donuts with the less-fattening center." I ordered two and tea; the former, served fresh from a deep fryer and the latter, in a hand-washed china cup.

While slowly enjoying this refreshment, I learned the proprietors, Gerald and Valerie Fuller, had been married nearly 50 years and had two children and six grandchildren. Gerald had been a grocery store manager and flew to the United States to visit supermarkets in the 1960s. Later, the couple owned and operated several stores, including the Creek Road Bakery. This beach kiosk was their — or was it his? — "retirement home."

Warming to conversation, Gerald was quick to share stories, which lasted through ales in two pubs and supper in the couple's home. Through it all, Gerald demonstrated a knack for blending truth with porkies and eyeing me keenly as I attempted to distinguish one from the other.

"You know those forts out on the Solent. You can see them

from shore, you know. Those are Palmerston's Follies. He was prime minister back in the 1800s during the French Wars, and they're called Palmerston's Follies because they were never used. You can buy one, you know. For a million pound note. They unscrew them every 25 years to let the water out. Left-hand thread."

He continued, "When the *Queen Mary* used to come into Southampton, when it came over the horizon and we were on the beach at Hayling, all the visitors would stand up and wave. Grannies would shout, 'Look, Mary. There's the *Queen Mary*.' But the locals would pack up their stuff and get back to the top of the beach because they knew in *exactly* ten minutes there would be a six-foot wave come in from the wash of the *Queen Mary* and all the sandwiches and buckets and things would get washed away. It was great excitement." Gerald chuckled. "That's true. I know, since I was on the beach."

He showed me a newspaper dated April 1, 1988. An article on the front page told of plans to build an entertainment establishment that would feature topless dancers and change Hayling's image of "Coasta Geriatrica." The article mentioned Gerald Fuller, of the Creek Road Bakery, as the person from whom shares of stock in the project could be purchased.

I asked Gerald how he got his name in the article.

"I wrote it!" he replied.

I looked at the byline — Joe Kerr.

"Joker," he explained. "Now that's a porkie. An April Fool, you know."

He handed me another newspaper. An article displayed a large photo of Gerald standing in front of his bakery and photos of four men, all small mug shots. "This is not a porkie, you know.

This is truuuuee. I had a shop on Creek Road. A bakery. In 1987, they had a general election, and it was in June. Well, that was the beginning of the tourist season here. So, I said to the wife, 'We've got to advertise. There's no good in people just finding us; we've got to tell 'em we're here.' The election was announced, and I said, 'Why not stand for Parliament?' And I did."

"You mean you ran for office."

"Right. Right. We call it 'standing.'"

"For a seat?"

"Right. Right. Standing. Anyway, it cost 500 pounds for the deposit, which I knew I'd lose. But a piece in the local paper — four inches by one column — is about 40 quid. You don't get many of those for 500 pounds, do you? And how many people read them? Naught, naught, naught one percent. But, I thought, 'Well, for 500 quid, you get free delivery by the postman for a leaflet to every household. You get your name on notices. You get a bit of TV coverage.' So, I called myself the Creek Road Fresh Bread Party because I had a bakery. This is not a porkie. This is true. My platform was 'Eat Fresh Bread Daily.' I got 373 votes. That's 373 dedicated customers.

"Now, you can see our election on TV — of what happens when the thing's announced. The one who wins stands up and thanks the police and everyone else. Then the next one has a go and slags off the one who won. The third one slags off him. And the next one. That sort of thing."

"Are you saying 'slags off?'"

"Slags off, you know. Has a go at them."

"You mean like taking a jab or a poke?"

"Yeah. That's right. Of course. We call it slagging over here."

"They don't just concede."

"Ohhhhh, nooooo!!! They *never* concede. They slag. This is England, you know. Anyway. The fellow who controls the election count is called the Returning Officer, and he came to me and said, 'Mr. Fuller, you don't want to speak, do you?' I said, 'Of course, I do! It's my last chance to aaadvertiiiiise!' I was the only one to get a cheer and a clap."

"Did you slag at the others?"

"Nooooo!!! There's no point in that."

"What did you say?"

"Oh, I can't remember now, but probably something like, 'I thank all the people who are seeing me here and hope that you all come to my shop and buy bread. I could use the money.' You know, something like that. But it's advertising, you know. They came to my shop. They bought bread. They talked about me. That's what it's about!!!"

Days later, after returning home, I logged onto the Internet and searched for "British Parliamentary Elections." There, I found a website, that credits Independent G. W. Fuller with an asterisk by his name and an explanation: "Fuller owned a bread shop in the constituency. He was the candidate of the 'Creek Road Fresh Bread Party.'" So, at least that part of his story is true. Now, as to Palmerston's Follies and unscrewing them to let the water out, left hand thread, well ...

What You Didn't Say

We talked late into the afternoon that Friday we first met, but we spoke little of your sudden dismissal from your job and the business project that had been the original purpose of our appointment.

We mused that, purposely, neither you nor I had described ourselves over the phone. You had simply suggested, "Noon at the Main Street Cafe."

Yet when you entered, I knew you. I stood. "Karen."

"Kevin."

When seated, you said, "This is my favorite table." You didn't ask, "How did you know?"

We quickly set small talk aside as though it was an unwanted menu, and we spoke of our lives, of unseen parallels. We frequently said, "Me, too," as we shared unwavering eye contact, gentle humor, and knowing nods.

And as I drove home through rush hour traffic, I thought about what you said — and what you didn't say.

You said you're 32, born in France, "swaddled in Army fatigues."

You didn't say 32 years ago was prior to America's bombing of Vietnam, a time when overseas military deployment was at Cold War levels. You didn't say that enlisted men didn't enjoy the privilege of having wives abroad and birthing children in military hospitals. You didn't say your father was an officer.

You hinted that you traveled during your youth.

You didn't say you never stayed in any one school long enough to bond lasting friendships, not long enough to fit in, especially in cliquey teenage years.

Your vocabulary spoke volumes, and you quoted Thoreau,

Emerson, and Shakespeare.

You didn't say classical authors were your best friends and that their adventurous passages carried you to faraway lands while your schoolmates partied.

You said you live "in the house where Dennis was raised." When you mentioned Dennis the second time, more than an hour later, I asked, "Who's Dennis?"

You said, "Dennis is the man I married 14 years ago."

"Are you still married?"

Your voice said, "Yes," and your eyes focused on the floor and spoke any number of messages that you wished it were not so — or different. These were not messages to me, neither a come on nor a tease. Rather your eyes spoke to the floor, and the floor spoke back to you with whatever message you desired.

You said you were married at 18 and spoke vaguely about his "proposal" and your "first date" and "maybe his first date, too."

You didn't say you had looked upon Dennis as comfort and stability, the young man with a castle, the Arthur of Camelot. Nor did you say he may have looked upon you as Guinevere, a beautiful woman with bright eyes and soft smile and fascinating stories who sailed from across the sea and into his life.

You didn't say Dennis was your escape from travel and snotty kids encountered in city after school along your path to early adulthood. You didn't say marriage and Dennis and Dennis' mom really became your entrapment in a life too comfortable, too routine, too stabile.

You said you were an introvert. Yet you also spoke of teaching and writing poetry. You spoke of joy you receive from giving, and your spirit said, "I am not an introvert. I have much to offer. Let me do it."

When the gentle jazz playing in the background took a bluesy turn to Billy Holiday, I looked at the empty hardwood floor beside our table and said, "Let's dance." I stood, facing you, hand extended — a gentleman's pose — waiting for you, a lady, to place your delicate fingers in my open palm. You brushed your long, dark hair aside and said "No" in several kind ways as I stood there, and all of them sounded like feeble excuses. I withdrew my hand only when you increased the intensity in your eyes and said, "I don't want to." After I sat down, you spoke softly. "I really would like to dance, but I would feel uncomfortable afterward. So I won't."

And you turned your eyes away again, toward the floor, and you whispered, "I haven't danced in a long time."

Cade's Cove

*I lay among wild daffodils
and feel a wild rush in my heart.
My shirt rides up,
exposing warm tummy flesh
to cold, damp afternoon dew.
I feel the heartbeat of the Earth.*

*Maples across the meadow
offer their buds, saved from killing
ice by 3,000 feet of de-elevation.
Up above, majestic frosted mountains
escalate in shadowed steps
to gray afternoon clouds.*

*The air is calm.
The sun suggests
the last rays of warmth;
but even a full day of suggestion
is not enough to melt
the mountain's icy cloak.*

*Yet, the entire scene will melt
a heart of mountain stone.*

Cosby Knob Shelter

Appalachian Trail – April 1, 1991

If I were an artist, I would paint this scene. I would sit where I am — at one end of the trail shelter, in the loft, my back against a sturdy, stone wall. On the right side of the canvas, I would paint the chain link fence that keeps the bear out and the clear plastic, now dusty, that only somewhat blocks the wind. The stone fireplace at the opposite corner of the shelter would be in the center of the painting, its yellow flames and orange glowing coals the only illumination in the room. Everything is near-black, except soiled white hiking socks hung on the line by the fire. Food sacks are strung like hams from the beamed ceiling. The people are silhouettes, standing by the chain link, crouching on the earth floor, or sitting on bunks that line the left side of the canvas. That's the scene, but it's only part of the picture.

If I were a sociologist, I would describe this group — seven Yanks from the Great Lakes Adventure Club and six Rebs from the Carolina Mountain Club. A baker's dozen with individual tastes for view and vistas who share a common spirit of adventure, exertion, and exhilaration. They are proverbial ships passing through life that happened to hike to the same stone harbor in the Smokies this night.

If I were a composer, I would capture the music — accent from the crackling fire, syncopated popping corn, and the gentle roar of a backpacker's stove boiling lemonade and vodka. The bass is the murmur of a half-dozen quiet conversations, "Ooohh" groaner jokes, backpacking stories, and "Yes, I'll have some more wine." A feminine southern accent solos, "I'm going to get me one good night's sleep tonight," while the G harp and ocarina provide melody and harmony — "Amazing Grace,"

"Good Companye," "Simple Gifts." A few voices sing along. Then, applause and intonations of "Wonderful" and "More."

Oh, yes, please play more. Play until conversations dwindle, the fire ebbs, and snoring signals a finale. For tomorrow, this will be a memory as 13 pack their gear, seven walk south and six walk north.

And such is the splendor of life that even if I were a painter, a sociologist, and a composer, I could neither paint, study, nor compose this event. No one person can. All 13 are necessary.

Each will leave with a different rendition and fond memory. Each will know in his and her special way that it was good — very good.

Pathways

I'm in the woods, hiking in the rain among autumn's trees, along high ridges and near cascading streams. What are you doing, Dad? Are you watching TV? Are you feeling all right? Is your medicine working for you today? No TV for me this weekend, please. I want to think.

Should I stay in the community where I've lived and made friends for 20 years, the community where my opportunities lie, the community of my business? Or should I return to the place I was born and raised, the place I once called home, the place where you want me to live?

No, I don't want to think about this, not right now. I want to enjoy the woods.

This area is all the way across the state from your old stomping grounds where you hunted deer when you were young, Dad. I wish you could hike this trail with me so we could walk together and you could tell me stories and I could tell you why I enjoy shooting pictures.

The trail is an 18-mile loop with hardwood ridges on the south side of a deep river valley and a vast stretch of low, marshy cedar bog along the stream's northern bank. My overnight destination, a primitive campsite, is eight miles from base camp if I follow the southern ridge; it's ten miles by way of the river's northern bank. Some people walk the extra miles in the first "half" of the journey, others in the second "half." It's like life, isn't it? A person can move directly from high school to college to marriage and family and old age, or take the longer route with pieces of retirement along the way.

The temperature is chilly this morning. The mid-October day is still young, and the sky is heavy with overcast as I break camp and walk through tiny pockets of sunrise, rain, and dropping temperatures. Fall color peaked last week, and branches of beech

and oak hold on tight to browning leaves while curved fingers of crimson maple float freely. Wind whispers through treetops.
　I have everything I need on my back: water, food, a tiny stove and fuel, my bedroll, tent, and clothing. The trick is to travel light, even with a camera and film. I carry my thoughts in my head.
　I should be with Dad. He wants me there.
　I don't want to move.
　Go.
　Stay.
　No, I don't want to think about this.
　Here's an interesting old maple, Dad. You'd like the history. There used to be a booming lumber trade here decades ago. Pine and hardwoods were timbered, hauled by horse to the top of the ridge, rolled, and floated in the river to the mills. One of the sawyers broke his saw and discarded it in the crotch of this maple, but the tree endured, covering the steel with its adaptive grain and protective bark.
　It was only three months ago, mid-July, when you told me you had Parkinson's.
　Do you want me to come back here and take care of you?
　I think that would be good.
　Okay, Dad.
　Moving seemed like the right thing to do then, but I think we reacted. That's why I had to raise the subject again.
　Dad, I can't move. I've been on my own too long. I think we'd be living too close.
　Do what you think is right.
　Are you disappointed?
　Yes. I was hoping we would do things together.
　Like what?

I thought you could shovel snow this winter and change light bulbs.

Dad, I'm not your 19-year-old handyman any more.

I wish you could see the view from the crest of this ridge. I'm looking over the crowns of trees rooted in the steep slope below. Through a single hole in dense gray clouds, the sun spotlights the distant forest and highlights lingering colors on the opposite side of the valley. The river runs like a silvery serpent more than 300 feet below. Wind rushes up the hill where logs once rolled and blows in my face. I close my eyes.

Please give me inspiration, confirmation, assurance. Tell me what's right.

It's raining, suddenly and harder than before. I remove my poncho from my pack and cover both it and me.

Can I carry your pack, too? Should I?

Parkinsonians in the support group have warned, "The more you do, the more dependent he will become."

"But he's my dad," I told them. "Maybe we could help each other."

"Do you really think so?"

Yes. Maybe. Although I would miss my friends. And I love the woods. And he says I backpack too much. And we disagree on religion. And he disapproves of my divorce, although being single makes it easier for me to move. And I don't want to move into his marriage or his generation. But he is my dad.

I'm descending from the ridge to where a spring-fed creek flows to the river. Cedar scents the moist air and I feel like I'm walking through mist sprayed from nature's wooden atomizer. Some trees stand tall, others have fallen in unsuccessful attempts to block the water.

My boots are black from sloshing through ooze that surrounds half-exposed roots. I'm trying to step only on roots, but occasionally I miss. This reminds me of being in first grade: sometimes I went straight home from school and sometimes I stopped to slosh in mud puddles along the way.

Upstream, where footing is more solid and the creek narrows, I've come to a footbridge. Standing on it, I lean my pack against the rail and become mesmerized by water rushing below my feet. A thin, translucent membrane rolls over a ridge of fallen sticks, then magically transforms into foam bubbles that dance like round silk fibers on a floating bridal veil.

The small cascade gurgles a constant symphony as each droplet follows another, unerring, unthinking, automatic in a predestined course.

"*Water flows downhill,*" *my geology professor often repeated. "That's all you need to know to pass this class." My geology instructor was simplistic.*

"*Life isn't simple anymore," you told me recently, Dad.*

Your mind is sharp. So is your wit. You have wisdom, in your own way, wisdom that works for you. Your medication is helping you breathe and speak better, and we've been talking and getting to know one another again. I like that. You've told me stories about Mom that I didn't know and about neighbors and friends and customers. You told me you loved your work, but you also said you felt like the "& Son" in your father's business. Every day, you followed in Grandpa's footsteps, like water flowing downstream. I'm a salmon, Dad, swimming against the current, resisting the eddy of my youth.

Where does that leave us?

I'm in the woods, huddled in my poncho, standing on a footbridge amid a forested, watery splendor; raindrops from above fuel the stream below. What are you doing? Are you puttering or dozing? Are you watching TV? Do you have the sound turned down or up? Nature sets the volume here; it's always perfect.

The Fence

The new neighbor, who had been the topic of conversation during breakfast, was on her verandah when we came home from the restaurant. Standing on a stepladder with her legs visible above the unpainted rail, she offered a first impression of bright yellow sweatpants.

"Do you want to talk with her about the fence?" I asked Dad while shifting their Chrysler into park and turning off the ignition. This is as good a time as any, I thought.

He didn't respond, and I waited, not sure if he was thinking or if he had decided to remain quiet or if he wanted to say something but was unable to because of the Parkinson's that shortened his breath and affected his speech.

Marie, who had been in the back seat, was already out of the car and walking toward the neighbor's house. I got out, closed the driver's door, and stood there, watching her and waiting for Dad.

At 80 and with gray hair, Marie moved slowly, at a pace she had been forced to accept since her heart attack six months earlier. She had lost enough weight during her recovery to go from a size 16 to a size 12. And at an inch less than five feet, her height was tiny compared to the three-story, century-old house that she approached. But she also walked tall, her stature gained, in part, from 35 years in a well-kept majestic house of her own. She was the matriarch of the block.

Dad rounded the car, his hand resting on the hood, giving him balance. He was still slender, about 150 pounds, the same as I. We used to be the same height, but now, I easily looked down on the top of his head. His hair was soft, white, and full. For that, I envied him. But he seemed to look shorter and more hunched each time I visited, the combined effect of age and gravity and carrying decades of worry on his shoulders.

You don't have to carry this one alone, I thought, believing in my naiveté that a simple conversation would resolve the dispute.

Dad took as deep a breath as was possible, then cleared his throat, a signal that he was preparing to speak. "I'm not sure we should talk about it on Sunday," he said in answer to my first question.

Ah, yes. An ancient Catholic theme, common to my upbringing, that was reinforced earlier this morning at Mass. Keep the Sabbath holy. Honor the day of rest. It was a theme of which I was reminded, as an adult, only when I visited Dad and Marie. But it was also a theme that I reaccepted readily — more out of love for my folks than out of devotion to doctrine. Yes, we won't discuss the fence now, but on some future *weekday*, I'll take time from work and drive back across the state, and we'll talk about it then.

The neighbor turned her head and lowered her arms, unhiding her face and dark curly hair. "Hi, Marie." She smiled and waved, then quickly climbed down the ladder and down the verandah steps, the last one of which led, not to a sidewalk, but to a deep trough that was layered with pea gravel and a few temporary stepping stones, waiting to be filled with fresh cement.

In her absence, the verandah was permitted to show it's own character: disarray and disrepair, camouflaged as work in process. It was huge, yet proportional for a house that probably, like Marie's, had 12-foot ceilings and thick walls with solid oak pocket doors. On that house, the white column the neighbor had been redecorating and its sole remaining mate — too large for human arms to fully hug — looked at home. The fresh pine two-by-fours that temporarily replaced missing columns looked like out-of-place sticks, like young boys with maturing spines suddenly thrust into the role of Atlas.

In the front yard, inside the fence, broken cement and fractured wood lay in piles at the foot of an ornate street lamp and hitching post — new, yet made to replicate circa 1890. If a carriage were to suddenly appear, it would surely be harnessed ahead of its horse.

"Happy Mother's Day," the neighbor said, now hugging Marie as the two women stood on the sidewalk between their respective houses.

Dad, still beside me, cleared his throat again, and I turned to face him as he spoke. "I'll get the survey." His voice was soft and raspy, and tentative. Then he climbed the steps of the home he had come to share with Marie and went inside.

The neighbor had her left arm around Marie's shoulders and was turning both of them to face in the direction she pointed with her right, drawing Marie's attention toward two houses across the road. "We're going to get them to replace the porches," the neighbor said. The houses were even larger than Marie's, and had been turned, by a nonresident landlord, into four-unit apartments. "So, they'll be just like they were originally."

"And over there," her voice bubbled with enthusiasm as she pointed at another apartment house that was the home of seven handicapped indigents, "they're going to replace the porch and get rid of that ugly thing," she said in reference to an enclosed outside stairway that had been constructed and painted to match the house's exterior. "They've got quite a problem," she continued. "They're fixing the roof while those people are still living there, and the workmen have to ring a bell when they climb the scaffolding so the people know they're there."

"Are they going to have to move out?"

"Oh, I don't know." She was now turning Marie, causing her to look at other houses in the historic neighborhood. "And everyone else is going to start painting soon. We've gotten a discount from the paint stores, and we're looking for old photographs of every house to see if we can find original colors, or at least color patterns." She looked at Marie with sparkling eyes. "This is so wonderful. The houses are going to be just like they used to be." She made it sound as though they had been neighbors for decades, not less than six months.

When the woman paused, Marie was finally able to say, "This is Martin's son."

"Hi," I said as I extended my hand. "I'm Bob."

She shook it. "I'm Violet." Then, to Marie, "And what color are you going to paint your house?"

Bright yellow, I thought, as I took in Violet's dirt-stained sweatpants, which were topped with a pale white sweatshirt. The clothes were large, but not loose and floppy. Her feet, clad in sneakers and white socks, were normal size, but her ankles were stocky. So were her wrists. And her black hair was pulled back to expose a solid, square face. She had high cheekbones, but not in the classic fashion of Cleopatra or Barbie. More like Dick Butkus. At 5 feet 4 inches, Violet could have been a female linebacker, or a welterweight wrestler.

"We're going to keep it cream and red," Marie was answering. "I want to change it, but Martin likes it that way." Her voice was gentle, loving.

"Well, I think you should make it more dramatic," Violet cut in.

Then, in the light of day, I took a closer look at her house and noticed what Marie had spoken of the night before. Six shades of purple, from lilac to lavender, or whatever obscure terms paint manufacturers and decorators use to describe obtuse colors. A predominant shade for the siding, but another for the fascia, and another for the trim. No, three shades for the trim, depending on where it was located, or depending on whether the trim piece was vertical or horizontal or circular. The shakes on the bottom row of the gable — and only the bottom row — were alternating shades of purple: light, medium, dark; light, medium, dark; light, medium, dark — like a narrow-band rainbow. The back porch was adorned with lathe-formed spindles; some vertical, some serving as spokes leading from an ornate semi-circular hub. The outermost vertical spindles were one shade of purple; the next two inward, slightly lighter; then two more, even lighter. Three shades in all — like the gable shakes — and all purple. All in a repetitive sequence. The spoke spindles and spool were old gold. The cupid weathervane was as out of character as Olive Oyl in Fantasy Land. And on the roof, occasional gray and rust red shingles had been used to create large petal patterns against a field of, yes, purple.

But the fence, both illegally and aesthetically out of place, was rough-sawn cedar with ragged splinters that would readily proffer slivers if casually touched. I would have expected black wrought iron with fake tarnish.

Dad approached with a piece of paper in his hand. I waited. After all, this was their dispute, and at midlife, I was only beginning to understand how our traditional parent-child roles were reversing. And Marie, the owner of her house and property, had said at breakfast that Dad, her "big boy," would take care of it. I waited and watched as Dad also waited and watched Violet's one-sided conversation with Marie.

Finally, she stopped and acknowledged Dad's presence. He stepped into the opening. "I want to talk about the fence," he said.

"Well, I don't know if we have time today. It's Mother's Day, you know. And I have to call my mom and stepmom. And Peter's working on the computer. We're going to call his mom and stepmom, too. So, that's four moms. Can you believe that? Four phone calls that we have to make. And they're all long distance. My Mom's in Quebec and my stepmom's in California. Peter's mom is on vacation somewhere, the Caribbean, I think. And I don't know if Peter is going to want to come out and talk to you about this right now, Martin, but I can ask him." To Marie, she said, "I think it would be great if you did paint your house a different color than what it has been." Then, with sudden inspiration, "Oh, I know what I was going to ask you. You don't have any pictures of our home, do you? As we fix up the verandah, we're trying to find out exactly what it looked like."

"No, I don't think so," Marie replied, drawn into the sidetrack.

Then, Violet was off again, talking about the cement railing on the porch, doubting its originality, wondering what it really looked like when it was new.

Dad looked — what was it? — helpless, but not helpless. Perplexed. Wanting to speak, but unable to do so fast enough. Unable to even clear his throat during Violet's brief and infrequent pauses.

Violet's arm was back around Marie's shoulders, turning her away from Dad. "Well, we were hoping that you might have some pictures. You know, of people on the verandah, or something."

I interrupted as politely as I could, "Violet, I know you said you're busy with phone calls today, but this fence issue is important to Dad and Marie. Do you think we could spend a few minutes talking about it?"

"Well, I don't see why we have to. I mean Martin gave his permission for us to put the fence where it is. And," she said, pointing to the house on the other side of her lot, to where the fence along the front sidewalk of her property turned at a right angle and disappeared, "we gave those neighbors two feet of our property so their place would look better. I mean, I don't see what the big deal is. We're just trying to do this for the neighborhood."

Diversion tactic, I thought. Trying to use one issue to set a precedent for another, unrelated, issue.

"But I'll ask Peter. I'll see if he has time to come out here and talk to you." She left, squishing pea gravel in the pit, taking a long vertical stride onto the first verandah step, then up and across the verandah, and into the house. The front door was a treasure hidden deep in the shade, darkened oak dominated by a tall oval of beveled glass.

I stood on the sidewalk. Dad rested against the top of the fence, his forearms protected by a long sleeve shirt and sweater. Marie walked away, leaving her two men to deal with the situation.

"Do you want me to speak on your behalf?" I asked.

"Yes."

"Did you give them permission to build the fence?"

"Not all the way out here. Just back there." Dad paused and cleared his throat.

Marie had overheard and returned. "Their back porch is only six inches from the property line. They asked if they could jog the fence around it back there. We didn't think they would bring it straight out all the way to the edge of the sidewalk."

"How much of your property is inside their fence?"

Dad started to hand me the surveyor's paper.

"Five feet," Marie answered.

I raised my eyebrows and whistled acknowledgment. The houses in this neighborhood were large. Six or more bedrooms, formal dining room, a sitting room, butler's pantry. Some had widow's watches. But the lots were small.

"The frontage is — " Dad started to say.

"Only 55 feet, 11 inches," Marie finished for him.

And the neighbors have taken 10 percent, I thought.

"She knows that what they did is wrong, too." Marie's voice was indignant. She was standing taller. "She pulled the surveyor's stakes out of the ground and threw them over into our yard." She paused. "But I don't know what to do about it."

"I don't, either," Dad said.

Marie sighed. "They seemed like such nice people when they moved in."

Violet and her husband Peter emerged from their house. She sat on the top step, flanked by a wide white support column on her left and a pair of pale skinny, almost bending two-by-fours on her right. Peter continued down the steps, into the pea gravel pit, then up again onto the sidewalk on which we stood.

"I don't understand the problem here, Martin," he began while still in stride. He was a big man, well over 6 feet. He stood close to Dad, too close. His thin curly hair was disheveled, his nose large. He probably weighed well over 200 pounds, and with a few more years of age, by about 45, his cheeks would become jowly. "Vi tells me that you've come over here to talk about the fence. That you feel it's in the wrong place. Well, you gave us permission to put the fence here. In front of your relatives, you gave us permission. You saw the holes that we dug. We talked about where the fence was going to go. And you gave us permission."

Dad took a half step backward.

"Now, Martin, you can move the fence if you don't like where it is. But I want you to know that those posts are cemented into the ground. You would have to cut them off with a Sawsall and rebuild the fence where you think it should be. But you would have to do that at your expense, Martin, because you gave us permission. I came over to your house during the holidays. You remember, don't you, Martin? And, there, in front of your relatives, you gave me permission to put this fence where it is. You can move it if you want to, Martin, but you will have to do it at your expense. You will have to pay about two thousand dollars." He began to repeat himself and didn't sound like he was going to stop.

Okay, how do I handle this? I thought. When do I step in? What does Dad want me to do? His eyes gave the answer that I had seen over the past five years, since even before the Parkinson's was diagnosed. It was the frustration of a keen mind and sharp wit physically unable to create verbal expression at will. Many times, I had waited patiently during conversations that took three times longer than normal. Often, I had said to Marie words that I now used on their new neighbor. "Peter, my dad would like to speak now." Then, I added, "Thank you for sharing your point of view. Now, let's hear what Dad has to say."

Practice makes perfect, I thought as Dad responded to his cue. "I said you could have space to walk around the porch. I didn't know you would build the fence on our property all the way to the sidewalk." He coughed slightly.

"But, Martin, what did you think? You saw the holes where we were going put the posts."

"You showed me holes by the porch. Not here." Dad put his hand on the frontmost fence post. His dander was strengthening his voice.

"But, Martin, you gave me your word in front of your relatives. Now, if you're going to go back on your word, — "

Dad deflated slightly, wounded, and I absorbed his dander, converting it into simmering anger. My dad had been in business in the area for more than 35 years. He was known throughout the county as a man of integrity. His word was golden.

Peter's words, in contrast, were repetitive, spewing in quantity for what they lacked in quality. More about what Dad "would have to do." More about Dad's word, given "in front of your relatives" and now challenged as unreliable. A guilt trip, I realized, and I stepped in.

"Peter, Dad doesn't have to do anything. *Your* fence is on *their* property."

Violet was on her feet, down the steps, and into the pit, her finger now pointing at me. "You stay out of this. This is between us and Martin and Marie."

I was taken aback, effectively shushed by an attack on my flank.

"Look, Martin," Peter began to make a transition from one tactic to another, "you can move the fence if you want to, but we can't afford to do it. This house is already costing us more to repair than what we planned."

Too many cans of purple paint, I thought.

Violet chimed in. "That's right. The roofer came to fix the roof and left a big hole just prior to a rain storm, and we had water inside. And we need to put in a new sidewalk here in front. And there's more cost to fix up the verandah than we planned on." And on and on. Another ploy: feel sorry for us.

For some reason I didn't immediately comprehend, Marie stepped off the sidewalk and into the pit of pea gravel. Her foot missed the first cement tile and sunk to her ankle. She wobbled, and I moved around Peter to grab her. But Violet was closer. She reached out and took Marie's arm, steadying her. Then, as Violet began talking to Marie, I realized why my stepmom had moved in that direction; Violet had beckoned her and was now leading her into a conversation about the color of her home: cream and red being discouraged in favor of something else. Divide and conquer.

Violet's voice was loud. Peter, though closer, was difficult to hear. I considered asking her to be quiet, but instead I listened more earnestly to the man. He was beginning to litanize. Finally, I spoke again. "Peter, your expenses are your problem, not my folks'. Let's stick to the fence — "

Violet looked at me, coiling to speak, not at all a shrinking violet.

"And, Violet, this is my mom and dad. I am involved." Happy Mother's Day, Marie, I thought, I've not often referred to you as Mom, even though you and Dad have been married for — what was it? — almost 14 years. I stepped around Peter and helped her back up from the pea gravel pit to the sidewalk.

"I don't believe this," Violet retorted as she stomped up the steps. "I don't believe we're talking about this." She stalked into the house, slamming the door behind her.

I prayed for the beveled glass as Peter launched into tactic number four. "Martin, we don't want any hard feelings here."

"Neither do we," Dad and Marie echoed.

"We don't want to raise this to an issue that can hurt people's health."

Like cause another heart attack? I thought. And I was glad I was there. To defend my parents from guilt trips, false precedents, diversions, and misdirected, unwarranted sympathy. To protect my parents' health from a youthful force they were too aged to face alone. So, this is what midlife role reversal is like.

Violet came back out onto the porch, shouting and repeating reasons why she and Peter shouldn't be talking about the fence, each one prefaced and closed with "I can't believe we're talking about this."

I can't either, I thought. Apparently so had Dad and Marie; she had already started to walk away, Dad was turning to follow.

"Look, Martin," Peter said softly, "we just want to be good neighbors."

I looked Peter in the eye and spoke with even greater softness. "Peter, good neighbors don't build fences on their neighbors' property."

There was silence, broken finally by Violet. "I can't believe this."

Eventually, the fence did come down, to be replaced, temporarily, by another. This occurred in late October. Marie had died earlier that month — from a second heart attack — and Violet had cried profusely, more than anyone else who had known her better and longer.

The new fence, of white wrought iron, was erected two feet farther into Dad's yard. Violet's claim, as repeated by the building inspector, was based on confusion about original plat surveys and discrepancies regarding whether the block was surveyed from 8th Street, to the east, or 9th Street, to the west. After more debate and consternation, Violet decided — for once, and for all concerned — that a compromise was in order: she and Peter would fence in only four feet of the original five they had already taken. Dad, tired of it all decided — for himself — that the whole affair wasn't worth any more sleepless nights and conceded.

In December, news spread throughout the neighborhood that Peter and Violet had moved out — suddenly. Stories abounded with dicey details about Violet changing the locks, throwing Peter's computer out a second floor window, and moving possessions out of the house late at night. Two weeks before Christmas, hired men disassembled the white wrought iron fence. Questions about where it was headed were met with discreet, vague replies. But within two hours, it was gone — all but the posts, both the wrought iron ones and the wooden ones — standing like skeletal sentinels in lightly falling snow, reminders of what was, what didn't have to be, and hopefully what wouldn't ever happen again.

The First Train

With anxious whistle
    blasting caution at every crossing,

we rush along the rails
    past blurring trees and poles

as my heart is pulled
    ahead of my body,

hurtling like a boulder over a cliff —
    but not fast enough —

to where my love waits,
    silent and steady, at the station.

The Third Train

The couple sat in his pickup in the village of his youth, a small village that featured one church, one post office, one bank, one grain elevator, one volunteer fire department, one closed cafe, and one pub. The western sky was growing dark with post-sunset clouds when the trains came rumbling out of the east, each one at a time when their conversation drew to a climax. The whistles and rumbles loudly forced the couple to sit in uncertain afterglow until the last car passed. She spoke of trains in movies, that they were metaphors for passage, transition, encounter, growth. He thought of Zhivago gripping the inside of his train's window as Lara passed out of his sight at the station.

Amtrak had brought this couple together six months earlier, in cold, snowy December. She had taken the train to him, and he to her. Once they traveled the rails together. That was the romantic encounter time symbolized by the first train — a time when things seemed smooth, delightful, and the lusty month of May lingered for six months.

The second train had the newest engines and cleanest cars. It crested the horizon in June as they neared their wedding date, when he moved back to his village, to be near her. It was the time when she readied herself for him and he thought he was ready for her. He wasn't, but the train was going too fast for him to see beyond the blur. She would stop him then and ask, "Do you still want to marry me?" "Yes, I do," he would reply. "Should we wait?" she would ask, seeking direction or confirmation. "No, I love you." And he did. And they wed two weeks before the third train cleared the turntable and rolled out of the station.

They sat in the village and watched it come out of the night as her face was lit by an ever more noticeable mercury vapor light.

A gray striped cat moved amidst tall weeds behind the cafe, scavenging for scraps. Patrons parked and entered the pub.

As the train raced through the village, the couple filled its empty boxcars and flatbeds with their concerns about newly discovered differences: her desire for a cottage in the woods, and his for a live-aboard cruising sailboat; her desire to make art from natural objects, and his to rid himself of all the "stuff" he had carried with him for too long — stuff in boxes and stuff in the leaden boxcars of his heart. She told him she had thought he was her Land Man, and he told her he had thought she would be his Sailing Buddy.

Then they reminisced their initial attraction, the writer and the artist who discovered each other on the first train. And onto this third train, moving fast out of town, he loaded his concerns about having too little income, and she loaded her fears that he would set her aside with the rest of his stuff. She loaded her love for him onto him, reminding him of the creative beauty he first saw in her. And he truly cared for her, moving the truck to get her out of the artificial light and into the light of reality and understanding and trust that would keep them on the same track together, ready for the fourth train. And the fifth. And on. Until they made their own train that would take them where they both wanted to go.

John

August 22

Dear Tom,
It has been so long since I have written or phoned you. So much has happened.
  John had a stroke. He can't paint any more. Thank God he is alive.
  It happened last November. I wanted to tell you sooner, but I didn't know how. Maybe I didn't want to think about it. Maybe I wanted to think about better times when I was pregnant with Andrew, when we all lived in Montgomery.
  We were like fish out of water down there with our mid-Western accents and John's strong Irish Boston brogue. "Page two," he always said. When he didn't want to talk about something, he dismissed it with, "Page two." I got so damn tired of hearing him say that. He can't talk now, not really, not without slurring. We used to lie in bed and talk till morning. We did that in college and when we were first married. Sometimes John would sketch. And he always had some beer and smoked those damn cigarettes. They didn't seem so bad then; I wish I would have made him quit. I want to talk with him now like we did then. About anything. I don't care what. I don't care if he swears or says, "Page two," or what. I just miss him.
  Do you remember when we moved to Alabama, Tom? 1974. You guys did so much for the marketing department. You wrote, and John and Lou did the graphics. Do you remember the weekends? You and Sharon would bring Justin and Jeremy out to our place in the country, and I would cook lasagna.
  We still have the illustration you and John did about how to find our place. Something about starting with the subject in

downtown Montgomery, driving through the verb until you get to — oh, you know, that thing that comes after a verb — and following the gravel roads and sand trails for 30 miles until you get to the dead end at the object of the preposition. I was going to put it up again after we moved to Gettysburg. It's framed. It's around here someplace.

You and John played volleyball, do you remember? You two were so skinny, and Sharon and I would watch from the house as you threw your bodies on the ground trying to keep that ball from landing. We laughed. It would not have bruised the ball to hit the ground once in a while. Sharon and I sampled the lasagna and watched you like other women watch hunks. You two were "our guys."

That was such a beautiful time. Beautiful country. John did some of his best painting there. Landscapes of pine plantations. Old Man Potter's place. That huge vice bolted to a fence post. That was one of my favorites. John put so much strength into the gray steel and the silver sun highlight on the knobby handle. I really wish, now, that we had not sold that painting. $300 seemed like so much money at the time, but I could use some of that steely strength right now. I feel like the rotten fence post, like the whole thing is going to crumble. And when it does, the vice will be the same, but I will be nothing. I wish I could be the vice. I wish I could look at that painting and pretend that I was holding the steel handle in my hand. To feel cool strength in the steel like John felt color in his brushes.

Do you still have the picture of Ollie, Tom? Do you still have her books and things you found by that old shack in the pine forest? Do you remember the tar paper siding and the cardboard walls? I know you remember. You have John's original. I hope you are doing something with Ollie's papers and books. Write about her. She is gone, and John could have been gone. "You only live once, and you're a long time dead." John said that over and over, and I hated that, too. I wish I could hear him say it again now.

He usually doesn't know me when I visit him in the hospital. I sit with him for hours. I talk to him. Almost every time I am there, he points at the nurse's call button. When the nurse comes in his room, he slurs the same old question. "Where's Karla?" he says.

"I'm right here, John."

And the nurse tells him, "Your wife is right beside you, John. She's been here all day."

And he tells her, "Karla. Never here."

John did a beautiful military montage near the end of Desert Storm. The original is an oil, 30" x 40". It has military heroes, men in uniform, and planes and tanks from all the U. S. wars this century. Patton and Eisenhower, the Marines raising the flag at Iwo Jima, World War II fighter pilots, and lots of other images. John said he remembered faces of soldiers in Vietnam and painted it for them. He hoped that when people saw men and women from so many wars they would say, "Enough. No more wars." We had 3,000 numbered prints reproduced six months before his stroke. They were selling well. We talked about a second printing. I don't know now. It doesn't seem important, and yet it is. I mean John's work is important, but I want my artist back.

They say he'll come back. After awhile, he can come home. I'll put a hospital bed in the living room. Can you imagine a hospital bed in here, especially after some of the Christmas trees we had? Do you remember the tree you and John cut and brought home in that yellow Vega? I saw that little rental car and I figured, at last, I would have a tree that didn't fill the entire cathedral ceiling. How much tree can you put in a Vega, right? I couldn't believe it when the two of you pulled in the drive. The tree trunk was on the dash, branches covered your shoulders, and the crown hung way out the back of the hatch. I just laughed and shook my head. John was bad enough. You two together were something else.

They say John will begin therapy before he comes home. They will put him on crayons and tracing paper.

Please visit us, Tom. John will want to see you.

Give From Her

David reached his hand from his sleeping bag and touched Vicki's shoulder. Her skin was bare above her sports bra. His touch was not soft, not direct, not firm, but fused.

"Take from her. Take from her. Take from her," he heard his voice say within his head. Though asleep, he knew what was to be take from her. The pain. The hurt. The injury of her accident six months earlier, in the summer, when she had fallen from her racing bike, trying to get away from the German shepherd. When she had scraped her face and shoulder for several yards along the macadamized surface of that Indiana country road. Without thinking, he knew this. Without being awake, he knew he knew this. "Take from her. Take from her. Take from her." The message was instinctive, basic.

Then it changed. His voice changed. No longer his baritone but a timbrous bass. "Give from her. Give from her. Give from her." He wanted to move his hand, but didn't, couldn't. "Give from her. Give from her. Give from her."

"Give what?" His silent question was a protest, a plea. He knew what had to be given.

Yet, the voice spoke. "Give the pain from her. Give the pain from her. Give the pain from her. Give from her. Give from her. GIVE from her." A command, gentle, firm, fused.

David's head shook violently. His neck wrenched. His right foot searched for, and somehow found, a small opening below the bottom end of the double-ended zipper in his mummy sleeping bag. He shook his foot, his leg, free. It touched a log that lay atop and below other logs, one of several that formed the cabin wall. It was cold. He was standing on a rock, on firm ground, overlooking a cliff with no bottom below. But he was okay. There, on firm ground. Grounded.

"Give from her. Give from her. Give from her." A comforting bass. A disquieting bass. "Give the pain from her."

David felt it run through him, through his hand, his arm, his shoulder, his body, his leg, his foot. Into the rock on which his foot stood. Through him. Into the rock. Over the cliff. To... where?

David shook his head. Shook it again. And again. His right cheek, then his left, slammed against the stuffsack into which he had folded his clothes and used as a pillow.

He awoke. The connection broke. His hand was hot, frozen to her body, frozen to Vicki's shoulder. He jerked it away, back. Back across the short gap that separated her mattress from his. Back to his own bunk. Back. Back inside his sleeping bag.

"Where did it go? What was it?" His voice was audible, a whisper. His voice, but it didn't sound like his voice. There was a croak, a creak, a crack in it. Drowsiness? No, he was awake. Wide-eyed awake. And scared. "What was it?" He was hoarse.

Without moving his body, without removing his right foot from the white pine log, he looked left, to the next bunk that stood frame-to-frame with his bunk, at Vicki. She lay asleep, her back to him. Her right arm and shoulder exposed to the cold night air, the cold Michigan winter air that permeated through the glass windows and through the crack under the wooden door and through the chimney of the wood stove that was now cool, if not cold, from lack of stoking. "Near morning," he thought. "Light soon."

He rolled over to his right, bringing his foot back inside the sleeping bag as he did so, back into cocooned warmth. He lay there awake, breathing deeply, trying to breathe normally, trying to figure out, trying to understand. Then, he felt her hand, warm, gentle, delicate on his shoulder. He heard her say, "It's all right.

Thank you."

He turned toward her, to acknowledge her, expecting to see her face, her eyes. But she lay as she had before, facing the other way, breathing steadily. Her right arm, the one on top as she lay on her left side, the arm with the injured shoulder, hung in front of her. Her right hand, both hands, were out of sight in front of her. On the other side of her body. Away from him. She could not have touched his shoulder. "But she did. You did." He wanted to scream the words, but didn't. His eyes bulged. Totally awake. "You couldn't have," he whispered.

He sat up then. With his sleeping bag still wrapped around him, he put his legs out the wide hole below the bottom of the zipper, slipped into his ski pants and put on his socks and boots. Standing beside the bunk, he pulled the bag over his head and put on his coat. He had to pee.

Outside the cabin, the waning moon shone bright through white pine. Brothers, no doubt, of the trees felled and turned into logs to make this cabin and the others here. His path to the outhouse was erratic. "Drunken sailor," he said, and an owl screeched from a branch, then became a dark spot passing between him and the moon. The cold ring of the outhouse seat on his butt and thighs jarred him more fully awake. He shook. "What was it? What was it?"

Back inside the cabin, he lit a candle on the wooden table and sat on the foot of his bunk, his back against the log that had been his grounding stone earlier. He looked at Vicki, asleep in her sleeping bag. Dan and Vera lay on the floor where they had placed a pair of mattresses pulled from two bunks.

"Was this what I felt when Vera called?" he wondered. He remembered the call to his home. Late afternoon. A Thursday. He had a client project to finish and deliver the following Monday. A weekend of work lay ahead. No big deal. No wife to deal with, not any more. No dates. Just the deadline.

Fortunately, Vera's invitation hadn't been for that weekend, but for two weekends hence. He wavered, not sure if he should take the time and was about to tell her "no thanks," when Vera mentioned her friend Vicki. She had done so, not to arrange a blind date, but, "She's just someone I think you should meet," Vera had said. "She's coming out of a bad time. Dan and I offered to get her away for a weekend, and we thought it would be good if you came along, too."

Even over the phone wire, David had felt a vibration. Yes, there was a reason to go. "Okay," he had told Vera, and they had made arrangements to meet at the Park & Ride along U.S. 131, at D Avenue, north of Kalamazoo.

He had driven six miles from his home to get there at eight at night and arrived a few minutes before they. "Not bad timing," Dan had said, embracing his friend, "considering we left home two hours ago."

The ride had been jovial. Four of them on one bench seat of Vicki's Ford F-150, heading north through Grand Rapids, Big Rapids, and Kalkaska under a star-filled dark, dark sky. Not crowded, not too cozy, just comfortable. David reconnecting with Dan and Vera, learning more about Vicki.

He was behind the wheel at midnight when Vera began the story about the dog. She and Vicki had been riding together a few miles from their homes when the German shepherd came racing out the long farm driveway at them. In spite of having spent nights alone in the Rockies, in spite of having been within yards of a grizzly, in spite of having crawled through chest-compressor passages in dark caves and having rappelled from the sides of mountains, there was something about the large dog that frightened Vera. "Everyone has something," she told her husband and friends that night. "For me, it's big dogs." Vera's voice lowered in volume. "We would have been okay if I hadn't swerved."

David took his eyes from the road to look past Vicki, who was sitting beside him, at Vera.

"My front tire clipped Vicki's back tire," she explained. "We both went down."

The telling of the rest of the story, by both of the middle-aged, wiry athletes had been intense. The speed with which they had hit the road, the slide, the scrapes, the sores. Walking to the next farm house, a quarter mile away, rather than retempt the dog that had lost interest and walked back to his own front porch. Calling Dan. Hours in ER. Vera's injuries healing, and Vicki's not.

"Yet, you wouldn't know it," David thought as he sat on the

foot of his bed, staring into the candle flame, then moving his eyes until they rested on Vicki's bare shoulder, still exposed to the night air within the cabin.

"You certainly wouldn't know it by the way she — they, the three of them — had skied into the cabin." It had been nearly three in the morning before they arrived at Wilderness State Park, within a half-hour of the Mackinac Bridge that connected the northern tip of Michigan's lower peninsula to the state's even more primitive upper peninsula.

Dan had been driving then and he had turned off the F-150's headlights as they entered the park. Certainly, they would be — and they were — the only ones on the single-track lane that led to the cabin parking lot. They had unloaded their gear from the truck to sleds and wrapped tow ropes around their waists. Then, they had put on their backpacks and headed into the woods to the cabin, their cabin for the weekend, a quarter mile through towering pines from the parking lot.

David was the slowest of the four, the most sedentary and most out-of-shape. Ahead of him, Vera led the way. Dan close behind her. Vicki, with long legs and at a little over six feet, had to slow her pace to not overtake the sled he pulled.

That night — last night, Friday night — he had chosen to sleep outside. For what was left of it. It was cold, but there was no wind. And the view from the cabin, through the trees, to the shimmering waters of Lake Michigan, illuminated by that time by a cream-colored moon, was too inviting.

With the rising sun, he had awakened and sat up. The winter dew had settled in and formed a thin layer of white ice crust on his navy blue sleeping bag. The stiffness of his moustache suggested his graying whiskers had also picked up a little more, if temporary, white during the night. But the view, the view that lay before him was so worth it. Lake Michigan. The beach stretching to the right, to the left, as far as he could see. Sand and snow in a caramel, vanilla swirl. Pine boughs dusted with sugar. Icebergs docked along the beach. Smooth ice stretching for hundreds of yards beyond them. The water, farther out, was flat, blue, glorious, inviting even in the cold. But he would not accept that invitation, for his nose picked up an aroma, sweet, pleasant, and fried coming from the cabin. Bacon, eggs, and coffee.

The first jaunt that day, Saturday morning, had been along the beach. West, toward where the tip of Wilderness came to a stony end. The rock formations there — some of them only one rock, some small islands with a few trees — stretched in front of them, reaching like bumps of brown sugar through the ice that surrounded them. The four pressed their cross-country skis forward, westward, to near the last island, to where the possibility of breaking through the ice became too dangerous to even consider. There, maybe ten miles from the cabin, they had eaten lunch, warmed by the sun that shone high in the southeastern sky. The blue was amazing, intense. The air, the freshest and healthiest any of them had breathed in too long. Gloriosity was beyond words, and they had spoken little.

The afternoon run was through the woods. On groomed trails, Vera shone with her skate-style of skiing, leaving herringbone tracks in a light dusting of snow that had fallen from trees as late afternoon clouds and accompanying wind had begun to blow in. By dusk, returning to the cabin, all were tired.

Then had come supper and the Indian Medicine cards.

David's head jerked as he realized he had been staring at them. There, on the table, in the glow of the candle. They were neatly packed in the box now. That medium-blue box that was a carrying case for the over-sized cards and the interpretive book that came with them.

But last night — this night, the evening side of midnight that was the apex of this same period of darkness — that deck, those cards had been spread on the table, illuminated by that candle, and the four of them — Dan and Vera and Vicki and David — had stood around them. Each took a turn at the tableau, each selected nine cards, arranged them in the proper order to represent nine directions — East, South, West, North, Above, Below, Within, Right, and Left — and turned them over one at a time as Vera read the meanings of each card, of each orientation — Up or Down, the "contrary" position that represents imbalance and lack of harmony.

He had gone first, David recalled, at Vicki's suggestion. She had fanned the cards in a near-perfect arc face down on the table and nodded toward him.

"How do I select them?" he had asked.

"One at a time. You'll know which ones to pick."

David had placed his hand, palm down, over the fan and scanned the array, passing his hand left, then right. With one complete pass, his hand began to quiver. He had felt something — cold, heat. He moved his hand back across the fan, slowly. Heat increased. Heat in his palm. Then, cooler. Then, cool. He reversed directions, back toward the source of the heat. Yes, heat. Yes. His hand passed over it, past it. Cooler. Come back. Heat. Stop. Steady. Hot. That one.

He bent his fingers and touched the card that lay below his palm. There was no heat, no sensation, in his fingertips. Not like there had been in his palm. He picked up the card and placed it face down in the spot where Vicki instructed.

"I felt heat in my palm," he had said. The others required no explanation.

And so it had gone for all nine cards, David recalled and realized he was rubbing his hands together in the cold night air of predawn. He pulled his sleeping bag up tighter around his shoulders, to his neck. The candle on the table ten feet away sputtered as a draft of air came from under the cabin door. A wisp of smoke escaped the yellow flame and wafted deeper into the cabin as though trying to outrun the draft. "You can't," David said and immediately wondered if that had been his voice, his thought.

He looked around the room. Vicki rolled over but remained asleep. He heard Dan — or maybe it was Vera — stretch and yawn, the sound coming from beyond the table. "Not yet. Not yet," he willed. "Don't get up yet."

The cards. The cards had been so right on, so right on for that moment in his life: The Crow, the symbol of Law, but his Crow was upside down, contrary, a symbol of the outlaw, of individual flight; Buffalo, the symbol of Prayer and Abundance, also down; Grouse, up, symbol of the Sacred Spiral, "leading us on to where we can live as one;" Beaver, the Builder, but turned down, an indication — an indictment? — that David had been thinking of selling his home and moving on; Turtle, the Mother Earth card, down, a sign, according to the interpretive book that Mother

Earth was calling him "to reconnect in some way;" and Frog, the Symbol of Cleansing, turned up.

Three had been blank, a phenomenon that Vera pronounced she had never seen before. "I'm in a time of change, of choices," he had told her. His choices for those cards had been a Zebra, representing black and white issues, no grays; a fast, powerful Cat, like a jaguar or lynx; and Trees because "no animals came to mind."

Six of Vicki's nine cards had matched his. Dan and Vera had an exact match, nine for nine, which he had found amazing, considering there were 53 cards in the deck. Most of theirs had been the same cards he and Vicki had drawn.

"What does it all mean?" he had asked then — what was it? Six, seven, eight hours ago? — "what does it all mean?" The question rang with relevance again now as a hint of sunlight began to show on trees and snow outside the window that stared back at him from across the room, from the across the flame. "What does it all mean?"

"David?" It was Vicki's voice. She rolled over in her sleeping bag and looked at him without raising her head from the mattress. She rubbed her shoulder.

"How do you feel?" he asked.

"What do you mean?"

"Do you know what happened?"

"When?"

"Last night."

Her head twitched and her eyes narrowed slightly, a cognitive reaction in her brow, as realization, a faint realization, set in. "No, I don't know what happened." She paused. "Do you?"

"No."

"But something did, didn't it?"

"Yes. How does your shoulder feel?"

Vicki brought her left hand across her body and rubbed her right shoulder. Gingerly at first, then with greater vigor. "It, it feels okay. Almost fine." She looked at him. "What happened?"

David hesitated, wondering if he should tell her. What would he say? He became aware of the log in the middle of his back, where he was leaning against the cabin wall. He took a deep breath and looked at her. "I reached over and touched your shoulder during the night."

She looked at him. More realization. "I ... think I remember that."

He nodded. "And I had a thought that I could take the pain from your shoulder. Somehow. It was like in a dream, Vicki, but I had that thought."

She smiled, but with far more curiosity than mirth.

"Then I heard a voice, a deep, bass voice." He hesitated, but the look in her eyes, locked into his, helped him go on. "It spoke like in a command. It told me to 'Take from her. Take the pain from her.' That's what I heard, Vicki."

"What did you do?"

"I felt it go ... through me. Then, I woke up. I was scared. It wasn't my voice."

Vera's head appeared over the table top. "Who do you think it was?"

"I don't know."

"Do you want to find out?" Vicki asked.

The question smacked David's attention back from the candle flame where he had looked upon seeing Vera come into his line of sight. "No." He hesitated. "I don't think so."

"Why not?"

"I don't think I could handle it. I couldn't handle the knowing."

There was silence in the cabin then. Vicki sat up in the bunk and rested her back against the upright post that supported the upper bunk. Her head was no more than four inches from the upper set of springs.

David asked her, "Do you want to know what happened? Do *you* want to find out?"

She rubbed her shoulder again, moving it, stretching it. "No, I don't think I do, either."

They looked at each other.

"Some things — " Vera began.

"Some things are better not known," Vicki interrupted.

David stretched his legs, which had been tight against his chest. "I don't think our answer, any answer of the daylight, could explain it. We would see things as we think they should be rather than the way they are, the way they were." After a moment, he added. "I honestly don't know what happened, but the only thing that comes to mind is — "

"Channel," Vera said.

He nodded, his eyes fixed on hers. "Yes. A channel."

"To where?" Vicki asked.

"I don't know."

"Does it matter?" Dan asked, getting up and moving next to his wife.

"No," Vicki said.

David shook his head. "No." He heard the voice, a timbrous bass, speak within his head. "No," it echoed, fading. And was gone.

Room to Play

The boy often went to his room early, before bedtime, because he wanted to be alone, to invent games he could play only in his head.

He had built the blue-gray wooden model of a PT boat that stood on its cradle on a small box in which he kept his underwear. The boat was almost two feet long, just right for his 12-year-old hands. He would pull out two D-cell batteries that he kept in the box, lift the deck to expose the insides, and set the batteries in their twin slots. Then he would flip the switch, watch the prop spin, hear it whisper whir, and pretend he was JFK winning the war in the Pacific.

Sometimes, he would lie on his back on the bed. With his left hand, he would touch the blue-and-orange Detroit Tiger pennant that hung on the wall. He would hold a baseball in his right hand, turning it slowly, running his fingertips along the seams, and imagine he was Al Kaline, throwing a runner out at the plate or driving in the winning run with two out in the bottom of the ninth.

He would lie there, smelling — almost tasting — the dust that collected in featherweight clusters on the barren hardwood floor under his bed and, which, sometimes, made him sneeze. He was aware of his weight on the mattress, and knew that if he moved too much, the springs would squeak and others would wonder what he was up to.

So, he would lie motionless and look around the room, painted in baby boy blue and barely large enough for the length and width of the twin bed. He would look at the boat on his right, at the pennant on his left, and beyond his feet at the small closet, not built into the wall but a construction afterthought with no clothes bar and no hangers. His clothes were inside — a jacket, two white T-shirts, and an extra pair of blue jeans – hanging on three nails, one on each wall. He couldn't see them, but they were there, waiting behind a faded cotton cloth that hung from a straightened hanger stretched between two more nails across the top of the closet opening. With his eyes, he would follow the dark wire back and forth, a wavy, imperfect pattern, like a road that goes from there to here. He would reach his hands above his head, wrap his fingers around the stiles of the iron headboard, and believe that, if given half a chance, he would come up with something better.

And that's when he would move to the corner of the bed, where the headboard partially blocked access to the only window in the room. He would curl his knees and sit on his haunches. He would raise the frame, prop it open with a cribbage board made from a mill scab of tree bark, and feel a northern breeze stir across his knees, up his legs, and under his shirttail. He would look through glass and screen and dust and dirt at two highways that crossed each other on the other side of an open field a half mile away. He would hear cars and semis and see lights flashing above the intersection, yellow and red.

On which road would five — or fifty — cars go straight through the intersection first? He would keep track on his fingers, bending them inward so the tips touched his palms: left hand for the north-south road, right hand for east-west. Which road would have more eighteen-wheelers while he counted slowly to one thousand? Which would have the first convertible in which he could hitch a ride? And which way would it take him?

Doll Room

I live in the Doll Room. John Wayne, the Duke, used to live here. So did Elvis Presley, Michael Jackson, Rhett Butler and Scarlet O'Hara, and Madame Alexander's numbered emissaries. They're gone now, passed on, like the Lady of the House.

The house is a three-story Victorian with 12-foot ceilings, walls two feet thick, and solid oak pocket doors. It has ornate wood carvings, decorative gold flake plaster, and glittering felt-textured wallpaper throughout. Everywhere, except the Doll Room. Here, the wallpaper is flat, dull, and torn, perhaps as old as the house itself.

My dad's bedroom is down the hall, but he sleeps downstairs on the couch. That's where he spends most of his days, either asleep or watching TV, following the action with glaucoma eyes but not knowing the plot. He listens to Dr. Joy Brown while eating breakfast and Paul Harvey during lunch, not knowing, five minutes later, what either said.

I understand there's a world beyond this. I've read about it, even been told about it. A chapel that's not really a chapel in Rome, a wall that's more than a wall in China, a waterfall thundering beyond imagination in Niagara, and another one in Africa. Rain forests, oceans, and snow-capped mountains. Countries that kill while professing peace. I want to go to those places, but am afraid to. I've never been out of the Doll Room.

Well, yes, I have. I've been to the pharmacy on the corner and the bijou across town, and I walk down by the river where tugboats push freighters out of port. I've watched mariners on the docks and truck drivers on the highways. I've read books that take me far into the past and far into the future. I even lived on my own, for a while, sort of. I could tell you about that, but don't want to.

I live in the Doll Room now. It's what might be called a back room in many houses because it's at the opposite end, and upstairs, from the front door, which, by the way, is locked with a skeleton key.

The only two windows in the Doll Room face south. The sun is nice until I notice dirt on the glass and shadows cast on the floor. On the carpet, actually, which is as old as the wallpaper, and as threadbare. Have the dolls been dancing on it when the Lady of the House wasn't looking?

She didn't look in here much. Except when visitors came. Then she would bring them to the Doll Room, and they would stand in the doorway or squeeze through narrow passageways and gaze in amazement. So many dolls. Winston Churchill, Amos and Andy, Abbott and Costello, Ken and Barbie, Charles and Diana, assorted nuns, and unnamed babies in carriages, cribs, and cradles. A quarter of a million dollars worth. At least. Bought one or two at a time, with no inventory records kept. Some of the early dolls, those placed carefully in the corners years ago, never saw the light of day once other dolls were placed in front of them.

Each doll had its own box, stored in closets in other parts of the house. But dust is a killer, so the dolls were housed in old glass meatcases or special oak cabinets with glass doors on the front and glass panes on the sides or inside glass fish bowls, irregular cubes of various sizes, which my dad dutifully stood on end. Each doll showcased, shoulder-to-shoulder with another, held upright by a metal bracket hidden under a skirt or up a trouser leg. Each one on display for no one to see. And certainly no one to play with; these dolls were above play.

They stood here, in fine attire, watching with fixed eyes, waiting. They served their life's role behind glass, not held, not touched, not read to, neither dusty nor dusted. Simply dolls. Quiet. Waiting. Watching. With no options to consider, no decisions to make. No places to go.

Kreager and Phelps

"All right, which of you wants to be Kreager?" the professor asked on the third Monday in September 1969. He was a big man, six feet four inches tall, and his voice boomed as he strode toward the small set. "Come on. Come on, now. This isn't a big decision. It's only a one-act play, and it won't make the networks," he said as he passed between two RCA studio cameras that, standing on their dollies, were taller than he.

When he stopped, the two young men were not three feet from him, yet they were in full illumination on the set while he was still mostly in shadows cast by the doors on overhead spotlights. They looked at each other, their silence punctuated by the clatter of an aluminum ladder as a lighting technician adjusted a backlight.

The younger student was a sophomore, nearly five inches taller than the junior, and he possessed the tapered physique of a tight end. The older student was slender, like a cross-country runner, and he would have liked to be Kreager, but —

Impatiently, the professor took a quarter from his pocket and pointed to the sophomore with his left hand. "Call it," he said as he flipped the coin with his right thumb, spinning it in a rising blur.

"Heads," the younger student replied.

The professor caught the coin in his right hand and slapped it on the back of his left. "Heads it is," he said. "All right. You're Kreager." He tossed the coin to him. "Here. You'll need this."

Kreager took the coin, looked at it, nodded as a slight smile curled his lips, and slipped it into his pocket, making sure there were no other coins in there, too. The junior, now Phelps, shrugged. Then, he and Kreager began to rehearse.

The professor returned to the back of the studio, to where one-inch black cables, the cameras' connections to electronic equipment in the control room, plugged into a sound-proof wall. He sat in a director's chair next to a shapely senior.

The made-for-television play was not a public production, but a live laboratory in which students practiced set design, lighting, wardrobe, props, and sound effects as well as acting. Those with a technical bent set microphones and ran cameras, videotape machines, audio control boards, and switchers. A student director called the shots.

The simple set created the illusion of a moderately cheap hotel with a single bed for each man. The headboards were backed by a flat with red and gold wallpaper, the pattern of which, with advanced imagination, resembled Greek urns. The bedspreads were solid gold and lay over plumped pillows. A table with a shaded nightlight and a black rotary-dial telephone separated the beds.

The room entrance was a door on stage left, hinged away from the cameras. On stage right, a small round table with an artificial woodgrain surface held an ash tray, matches, and a TV program guide. It was sandwiched between two cloth-covered chairs. Near it, a television set was perched on a platform suspended by invisible wires. A metal coat rack, complete with wooden hangers, was near the entrance door. Beyond that, a bathroom door was ajar. The bathroom light was on.

"Quiet on the set. Tape is rolling." The command came from a student floor director who crouched between the cameras. A red tally light atop Camera 1 came on. Camera 2 dollied right a few inches, and the boom mic operator modified her position, also.

Phelps, dressed in a navy blue suit, entered the room and claimed the nearer bed by placing his attaché and suitcase on it. He opened his luggage and began to remove business and sports attire that wardrobe students had packed into it and which, if he had tried to wear, would not have fit. He was standing by the metal rack hanging a suit when Kreager entered. "I'm Phelps," he said, extending his hand.

Kreager shook it. "Kreager." Then, seeing the first bed already taken, he crossed the stage and set his suitcase and valise on the other.

Phelps sat on his bed and leaned against the headboard. The

papered flat shook slightly. "Where you from?" he asked.

"Evanston," Kreager replied, beginning to unpack. "And you?"

"Decatur. Were you just hired, too?"

"Yes."

"Do you like it so far?"

"So far. I think I'll do better after this training."

"Me, too. I've only made three sales so far."

"I've made five," Kreager boasted.

Their conversation finally turned from exaggerated claims of expected wealth to what they might do on their first night in town. They dismissed looking over new product literature and watching TV, considered hanging around the hotel lobby or hitting the bars, and finally, at Kreager's suggestion, they decided to get laid.

Phelps said he had a friend in town and made a call. From an imaginary person on the other end of the line, he got a number and made another call. Then another. And another. He was down to the fifth somebody who knew somebody when he connected, speaking half of the phone conversation while Kreager stood with jockey shorts and socks in hand, listening, anticipating. When he hung up, Phelps said triumphantly, "She said she lives just around the corner. She'll be right over."

"She? She? You mean, by herself? Just one?" Kreager asked in a voice so strong that the audio technician in the control room rode the sound pot to modulate the recording volume.

"Well, she might bring a friend, but she wasn't sure," Phelps said, trying to sound sure.

"Oh, that's great," Kreager intensified. "That's just great. No. She'll show up alone. I see how this is going to go."

"Well — " Phelps tried to interject.

"Hell, man. I didn't come up with this idea so you could get laid and not me." With a large overhand swing, Kreager hurled his shorts and socks downward into his suitcase. "What am I supposed to do while you're up here with her?"

"Well, maybe, she and I could go back to her apartment. You know, we could take off and — "

"Maybe *you* could take off alone and leave *her* with *me*," Kreager bellowed. "How's that sound?" He moved three steps downstage and around the edge of his bed, threateningly toward Phelps. The younger actor's physique and voice fit his part, proving the coin had cast well, and, for that, Kreager rewarded it with a cameo appearance. He reached into his pocket and produced the fourth character that spoke no lines but would play the deciding role. "Heads I get laid and tails you get lost. Got it?"

Phelps was silent.

"Good. 'Cause that's the way it's gonna be." Kreager flipped the coin, letting it fall and bounce on Phelps' bed. Camera 2 zoomed in to the spot on the spread where silver glistened against gold. Heads.

There was a knock offstage.

Camera 1 had the wide shot.

Kreager swiped the coin from the gaudy bedspread, went to the door, and swung it open with male bravado. He eyed the third character, the shapely senior, up and down, as she stood in the doorway. Then, he presented the coin, held by the fingertips of his left hand, to her.

She took the coin, sashayed onto the set, and crossed downstage from Phelps, who still stood by the phone between the two beds. She raised her left arm and skimmed her fingertips across the TV stand, as though checking for dust, which lifted the hem of her black miniskirt. The floor director crouched low and leaned right to catch a glimpse of a silver garter near the top of her left stocking.

With practiced nonchalance, she turned away from the cameras before alighting on the foot of Kreager's bed next to his still-open suitcase. She glanced at his skivvies while rolling the coin in her left hand. She looked at it then and held it motionless while Camera 2 picked up an extreme close up. She rolled it over slowly, letting the camera, the videotape, and everyone watching a monitor see what she had seen — the profile of George Washington on both sides.

"Close up of her on 1. Ready 1. Take 1," the student director said in the control room. Camera 1 came on a moment before she lifted her head and smiled at Kreager, who was still holding the open door.

Camera 2 came back on, now on a medium shot of Kreager.

He was looking at Phelps.

"Zoom out, Camera 2. Give me a wide shot."

Phelps looked at the girl, the girl he had found, the girl he had called. She turned her right shoulder and head toward Phelps and arched her back, revealing the top of her half-exposed breasts to him. He looked down at them, at her.

While watching Phelps' eyes eye her, she crossed her black-stockinged legs at the knees, left over right, revealing most of her left thigh and silver garter to Kreager who was still holding the open door and, now, looking at her legs, at her. "Well..." he said to Phelps with more Ls than necessary.

Phelps, following the script, counted to five, then stepped through the line of the other actors' gaze and exited through the open door. Without looking at the shorter actor, Kreager swung the door shut behind him and swaggered slowly toward center stage as Camera 1 followed him and slowly zoomed in.

"Continue your zoom, Camera 1," the director called. "And, now, slow fade to black."

The technical director moved the fader on the control panel, and monitors showed blackness spreading inward to a small circle in the center of the screen that revealed Kreager's hand reaching the provacative female knee.

Minor applause echoed in the studio as the professor boomed, "Okay. That was good."

Throughout the semester, Kreager and Phelps and other students played various roles, took on different studio assignments, and watched obscure productions, some written by students in creative writing classes, that would never even earn a rejection slip from NBC, CBS, or ABC.

In the meantime, politicians and generals manufactured scripts of war that played across America and into southeast Asia. Young men went overseas and came home in caskets that veterans of earlier foreign wars ceremoniously draped with flags. Families cried in graveyards as unwitting soldiers played taps and gun-saluted blanks into the air.

On December 1, 1969, young people stopped spinning their Moody Blues and Jimi Hendrix and Willie Nelson and focused on one sound, on one show — that of birth dates being drawn from a drum on national television. Students in every dorm on campus gathered in front of TVs and listened and watched. Young men and women in every college and university in the nation listened and watched. Families and girlfriends and fiancées listened and watched.

In the communal TV room in Phelps' dorm, men, most not old enough to vote, sat on couches, chairs, and on the floor. They leaned against support posts and walls with bulletin boards laden with campus posters and notices of stereos and books for sale. They stood alone and in clusters. They listened to the invocation of what was a unique, somber ceremony — a rite of passage to a distant land and potential death.

Then it began. New York representative Alexander Pirnie of the House Armed Services Committee drew the first capsule containing a small piece of paper. "September 14."

"Oh, shit," responded one soft voice from a couch. A hundred male faces and those of the coeds turned toward the student who had spoken. They watched him get up and stomp out of the room. Except for a lingering memory of those two words, which hung like an epithet on a hook to be reused by others later, the room was quiet.

The Lottery continued, with each of the remaining 365 capsules drawn, one by one, by young men and women of the Selective Service's youth advisory committees, peers of 18- to 26-year-olds from around the nation.

"April 24."

"Has it started yet?" someone asked as a handful of students entered the TV room.

"Yeah."

"Shhhh."

"December 30. February 14."

A coed, standing in front of Phelps, clung to her boyfriend's arm. Across the room, another couple nervously held hands; a diamond sparkled from hers. A freckle-faced freshman sat on a beanbag and prayed a rosary, his fingers moving the beads and his lips mouthing repetitious litany as, on TV, Selective Service Director Lt. General Lewis B. Hershey watched birth dates be drawn and horoscopes rewritten.

"October 18. September 6. October 26. September 7. November 22."

"No."

"Is that yours, man?"

"Yeah."

"Geez, I'm sorry."

And so it went until the 366th date, June 8, then the 26 letters of the alphabet — J first and V last — were drawn and called. The live program ended with a benediction. Then, silence became chaotic conversation, crescendoing with whoops of relief while the unfortunate stiffened with consolation. Nobody bothered to shut off the TV as network commentators diagnosed the situation, unable to see from their electronic cloister the faces of American youth on the receiver side of their cameras.

On the last day of the fall semester and a week before Christmas, cold temperatures caused mid-westerners to bundle in heavy coats, and large snowflakes threatened to live until spring. Phelps had the heater turned on high as he drove his '59 Buick LeSabre down a hill near campus. He reached for the radio to crank up The Doors when he saw the hitchhiker who stood with his right hand exposed, his thumb extended toward traffic.

Kreager saw the car pull over to the curb and others change lanes to avoid it. He picked up his huge stuffsack and lumbered toward the Buick.

Phelps reached across the seat to unlock the back door on the passenger side. Kreager opened it and tossed in his bag.

"I almost didn't recognize you," Phelps said as Kreager swung into the front seat.

"Yeah. I'm glad you stopped."

"Where you headed?"

"Canada."

Phelps looked at Kreager. "What's your number?"

"Fourteen."

"Oh, shit." Phelps turned the radio off. It was not a time to light anybody's fire.

They rode in silence. Canada was 300 miles away.

"I was only going downtown," Phelps said, "but I can take you to the highway. Jesus, man. I'm sorry."

"Yeah. Well, you know — "

"Fourteen?"

"Yeah."

"I could take you a little farther if you want," Phelps said as they neared the highway. "To the next town?"

"Naw, this is good. There's lots of traffic here."

Phelps braked the car and Kreager got out. He hesitated after getting his gear from the back seat and before closing the rear door. "What's yours?"

Phelps looked at him. "Do you really want to know?"

"It won't change mine."

"Two hundred ninety," Phelps said after a moment's hesitation. "I guess you'll be stayin' in school?"

"Yeah."

Kreager shrugged and closed the door. He turned and walked away, across the highway to the northbound lane. He stuck out his thumb.

Vegetable Beef Soup

Joe signed his name. Yes, it was the right thing to do. He was sure. He was doing it for his wife, the UWC, the Reformers, the Veals who would become Pages. He looked down at the signature. His signature. He felt the quill pen in his hand. A queer feeling, that quill pen. Ironic that, in this time of electronic exchange, permanent ID, and personal history chips implanted in the back of the ear, they gave him a quill pen to sign his name *for this*. They had given him a bottle of ink, too. Real ink, like he had heard his grandmother speak of. And a quill pen. And, yes, even a piece of paper — he hadn't seen paper in years. He had signed his name. It was scrawly writing. He hadn't held a pen in more than a decade, and that one had been a stella he had used to sign an electronic mag pad when receiving a package at the UWC. But this signature was different. He was about to deliver himself.

    The doctor opened a locked room, clean and sterile but locked like a cell, and introduced him to the five youths whose lives Joe would change. Joe recognized their mixed appearance, men born of lust and into labor. Veals, named after the caged cattle they slaughtered. They were the current special project of Reformers who converted them into Pages for the UWC, which now employed over half the world's population. But the conversion was not psychological or even elemental. And certainly not astrological. Those practices — first Freud, then Jung, and later Chopra and New Agers who preached unlimited human potential — had been set aside, cast aside, in favor of injections.

    Injections cured everything. What used to be known as the common cold was wiped out in 2002. Cancer, all forms of cancer, a year later. Diseases of the skin, Parkinson's, Alzheimer's, Crone's, Lou Gehrig's. All of them gone, wiped from the face of the earth. Average age statistics were out of control now. Life expectancy had skyrocketed, and the only sure way to die now was by choice. Injection.

Joe looked at his signature. He held the quill pen. He rubbed his hand across the paper. He was ready. To go. The old fashioned way. Like Socrates. Hemlock.

The doctor took the paper from Joe's hand and spoke the names of the five young men. He told them that this man, Joseph L. Nobi — the doctor called Joe by his full name — had just pledged his life for them. The doctor asked each one if he understood the significance: no more crimes, no more eating raw flesh, no more lust. He told them that an injection from Joseph L. Nobi, as he died, would convert them to a life of service. Joseph L. Nobi's blood, the doctor told them, would make them better men. For society. For the UWC.

They said they understood. But the doctor placed his hands on their shoulders, looked them square in the face, and reminded each, in turn, that if they went back to a life of crime, even a minor thought of passion, they would immediately die. Alarms in their implanted chips would sound, and they would be brought before a judge, and the sentence would be death. By injection. For them, he told them, there would be no turning back, no leniency. Because they had made an agreement, their final deal, the ultimate plea bargain — to receive the Good of a Good Man. The doctor pressed his final words, squeezed them into their shoulders.

Joe Nobi felt good. He *was doing* the right thing. His entire being knew that. All except the small twinge that played and danced right behind his belly button. But he had come to accept that feeling; he had had it for so long that he hardly noticed it any more. Funny that he noticed it now.

Joe Nobi wondered what would happen next. He had heard of others who had done this. A friend of a friend had told him of a friend who had done it. That's when Joe Nobi first got the idea. It was right after he had begun to feel his wife didn't want him any longer. That's when he had decided that giving himself to society was the better course.

It's about time, he had told himself, to do something worthwhile. He had tried art when he was young, but that didn't work;

he liked art wherever he saw it, whether huge paintings that covered skyscrapers or the work of old masters in museums, but he couldn't draw. He had tried poetry, but no one ever read his work; besides, every street corner had a poet tossing verse into the air like bread crumbs for pigeons. He had tried wit, but no one practiced wit anymore, and people looked at him in a strange way when he told a joke; eventually he forgot punch lines that once curled his lips and massaged his mind. So he had studied cultural law and entered the UWC as a Page Master. That was when he had first noticed the twinge behind his belly button.

He had laughed at his use of the phrase "belly button" then. Now, as he walked down a long sterile corridor with the doctor, the term came bounding through Joe Nobi's consciousness and he almost stumbled. Belly button. My god, that was an archaic term. And where did it come from? There was no button in the belly. What were the other terms people used to say? "Innie" and "outie." He put his hand over that center part of his anatomy, over his abdomen. His palm against his tunic calmed him, as if he had placed his hand over his mouth to smother a snigger.

He quietly complimented himself. To snigger would have been impolite. In the chambers of the UWC, it would have caused others to sneer, then later he would have received a reprimand. No, no belly buttons, not anymore, Joe Nobi reminded himself. Yet, what was it? There was something inside, deep inside, that felt hard. His mind saw a large mother-of-pearl button that his grandmother had shown him — it had been made by his great-great-grandmother from the shell of a clam, harvested from a river over a century ago — and now, in his mind, he saw it as a growth protruding from his innie.

The doctor stopped next to a closed door, one of many they had passed in the brightly lit tunnel, somewhere deep in the clinic. The doctor looked into a laser beam that scanned his retina, and an elevator door slid open. The doctor and Joe Nobi entered, and the doctor spoke the number 14. The elevator descended. Did Joe Nobi feel something rise inside of him, deep behind his navel? He suppressed his desire to think "belly button."

The doctor asked Joe Nobi if he was all right. Joe Nobi gave the prescribed answer.

When the elevator stopped, the doctor stepped out first and Joe Nobi followed. He could hear only the noise of computer hum. How odd, he thought. White noise used to be the sound of rushing air. And before that, it was sterile music. Recorded computer hum became popular the year before the millennium, Joe Nobi remembered, when the natural volume of computer hum was reduced to legislated levels. Later, white noise companies began to market recordings of soft, but nondescript, human voices. Voices to mask voices. From somewhere deep in his memory, Joe Nobi heard water hammer. He looked around at the gray clinic walls, half expecting to see an ancient silver steam radiator, like the one that slammed into his waking consciousness on youthful winter mornings at his grandmother's house. A smile escaped him.

Suddenly, he became aware of ringing in his ears. It was low at first, inside us, but grew in volume as he tried to focus on the sound of the computer hum. So, he had it, too, he said to himself. Until now, he had never been sure. What was it — two, three decades ago — the Multi-Pros, Doctors/Lawyers/Politicians, within the UWC discovered that ear ringing was the best way to drown out unwanted human conversation. So all the walls of all buildings had been retrofitted with speakers that emitted a constant searing, ringing tone. Joe Nobi heard it all the time. At the office. At home. On the tram. He had thought it must be coming from the walls, the speakers. But now, amidst hum in the clinic hallways, he heard ringing. And it was coming from his own ears!

That was fair, he told himself, feeling quite professional and matter-of-fact as he strode evenly next to the doctor and remembered each of his four promotions within the UWC. The tinnitus project had been one of Joe Nobi's noblest accomplishments, a move toward equality. "The Glorious Tones of Tinnitus." For everyone. How had this hallway missed the conversion?

The doctor entered a room with a double helix stenciled on the door. Joe Nobi followed. A woman came toward him and, without introduction, began to explain the injection. She showed Joe Nobi a long syringe needle attached to a clear vial. She pushed the plunger and a drop of clear liquid emerged and hung from the end of the needle. She coaxed the drop onto her forefinger, then rubbed it on her thumb before wiping it into her apron.

Joe Nobi caught his breath and swallowed. The woman said he could have a stethoscope if he wanted to monitor his own heart beat, right up to the point of unconsciousness. She said a lot of people like to do that. An interesting experience, she called it. Like returning to the womb. Joe Nobi said that would be nice. He unconsciously draped the stethoscope over his arm as though it were a jacket removed on a warm spring day.

The woman came toward him with the needle. Joe Nobi stopped her. He asked if he could have an extra minute. The doctor looked slightly surprised, but he had heard the request before, so he nodded his head. The woman stared impatiently at Joe Nobi. Then, three seconds later, turned away and said the doctor should call her when they were ready.

Joe Nobi asked the doctor if he had a choice of when he could receive the injection. He heard his voice as gravel and felt as though it were coming from below his belly button. The doctor said that *was* unusual, but since Joe Nobi was a respected member of the UWC — wasn't everyone? — he could take the syringe with him and give himself the injection whenever he wanted. But he must return immediately afterwards, the doctor said sternly, so the Veals could receive their injection, too. The injection of Joseph L. Nobi.

Joe Nobi said he would, and the doctor called the woman who, with great skepticism, showed Joe Nobi how to insert the needle into his own vein. She made him push up his tunic sleeve and practice — twice — with a second needle and syringe that, she said, contained only sugar and water.

Outside the clinic, Joe Nobi caught a surprisingly empty tram and rode through the city. His ears rang. His eyes held the skyscape, lit throughout the day by artificial light. His hands held the syringe, its needle unprotected from the air. Fortunately, Joe Nobi reminded himself, there were no germs. They had been wiped out with the Great Eradication of 2011, two years after the last weeds and algae had been destroyed. He remembered a book, *The Mugwumps*, he had once read to his children about plants and weeds that went underground for centuries while humans covered the earth with concrete and asphalt. Then the vegetation, the Mugwumps, slowly began to emerge and push up through cracks in the concrete crust until they tore the slabs to bits and dust and, again, ruled the Earth. Joe Nobi wondered what had happened to his children. Where were they? And what were their names?

Suddenly, Joe didn't want to die. He wanted to ride in a car, his own car. A Ford, with his wife at his side, like they used to do. He wanted to feel hand-dipped ice cream on his tongue and an old-fashioned pointed ice cream cone in his hand. He wanted to eat Campbell's vegetable beef soup from a ceramic bowl, with a spoon.

He could see the bowl, light brown and rounded to fit the curve of his cupped hands. His grandmother had owned such a bowl. She had taught him to hold a spoon so as not to spill soup as he lifted it to his mouth. She had told him it was impolite to drink soup from a bowl and to make slurpy sounds. Joe Nobi made a slurpy sound and surprised himself. He looked around the tram. No one noticed. Tones of Tinnitus were louder than his slurp.

Then Joe Nobi thought of his wife. He saw her as a large woman. Very large. Too large to lie on top of him as they had once done while conceiving their children. She was taller than he, over six feet tall, with large, wide shoulders as wide as her hips. She wore long skirts that swept to the floor and long, buttoned sweaters that draped her shoulders and hung to her knees. Joe Nobi could see her walking several feet in front of him, as she often did, when they were out in public. Except for her head of white scraggly hair, she was a tall, swaying, ambling rectangle, bedecked in green, orange, and pale yellow-white.

He looked at the syringe in his hands and saw peas and diced carrots and potatoes swimming in golden, greasy broth that he stirred with a spoon in search of tiny bits of beef. He saw one. He herded it toward the side of the ceramic bowl. He loaded it onto his spoon. He brought the spoon to his mouth. He injected his tongue.

Joe Nobi yelped. He looked up. People looked at him. The tram stopped. Joe Nobi got off. He was in front of the clinic. He raced inside. His wife was there. She was lying on a bed. Tubes were attached to her legs and arms, to her large abdomen and wide shoulders. The tubes reached out to humming machines laden with blinking lights. He said, "What are you doing?"

"I'm having my veins fixed."

"Why?"

"So you will love me again."

"Why didn't you tell me?"

"I wanted to surprise you." She winced with pain. Then smiled, slightly, unsure.

The doctor was sitting on a step near the foot of the bed. He held his head in his hands. Slumped, his broad shoulders looked too large to be real. Quasimodo, asleep. Joe Nobi touched the doctor's shoulders. The doctor didn't move. Joe Nobi shook the doctor. The doctor grunted. Joe Nobi squatted in front of the doctor and bent his torso to put his head below the doctor's, to turn his neck and look up into the doctor's face. The doctor opened his eyes.

"How much time do I have?" Joe Nobi asked.

"What?"

"How much time?" he practically screamed.

The doctor looked blank.

Joe Nobi grabbed the doctor by the shoulder. Somehow, he seized the strength to move the doctor up off the step and past his wife and out of the room.

"Can you make it stop?" Joe Nobi demanded.

"I can't."

"But my wife — "

"I know." The doctor shook his head. His eyes cast down, ashamed.

Joe Nobi's shoulders dropped. His face sagged. The mother-of-pearl inside his belly fell. "So that's it?"

"I'm afraid so."

Thanksgiving at the Parisville Bar

Stories are supposed to have conflict. This one doesn't. Well, the Lions beat the Bears at the Silverdome 55 to 20, but that's about as tooth-and-claw as this story gets. Saddam Hussein was barring U.N. investigators from looking for biological and chemical weapons in Iraq, but that was half a world away and could be removed by flicking a button on a television remote control. Outside, an occasional shotgun barked probable death for a still-rutting buck, but that, too, was muffled and distant.

No, this story is about three people who shared Thanksgiving at the Parisville Bar. One was a man of 82; the second, a woman of 66; the third, another man, 50. Each 16 years younger, or older, than another. Their ages arranged like the smooth rise and fall of a sine wave. Semi-generational symmetry. Not conflict.

Parisville is in the cuticle of Michigan's thumb, 14 miles inland from Harbor Beach, the hangnail on the Lake Huron side. Nearby towns include Ruth, Ubly, and Bad Axe. I suppose if you want conflict, you could go there and research the origin of the name. Explore questions like "Who's axe?" and "What was so bad about it? Did it have a broken handle? A dull edge? Or was it used to kill someone?" Ubly has a drag strip, the noise from which, on a still summer evening, can be heard a dozen or so miles away. Ruth? No, no conflict in Ruth, a place with giant grain elevators and a small population of peaceful farmers.

Parisville is even smaller. There's the bar, founded in 1876, sitting on the southeast corner of two two-lane country roads. It used to be a hotel, stagecoach stop, and automobile and farm implement dealership; Henry Ford slept there. There's an abandoned auto repair shop across Ruth Road to the north and a house across Parisville Road to the west of that. A dance pavilion once graced the fourth corner, but it's gone now, burned decades ago. St. Mary's Catholic Church and a few more houses sit quietly a quarter mile away. You could fit the whole affair under the Eiffel Tower, with room to spare.

Now, I will admit that these three people have experienced conflict and sorrow in their lives. Look at their ages: 82, 66, 50. These are not innocent babes, not like the McCaughey septuplets born eight days earlier. Martin lost his second wife in October to a heart attack, his first wife 31 years prior to cancer. Bob was divorced and struggling with a tumultuous relationship. Lorraine's husband died four years ago; he had lost two fingers on his right hand in an industrial accident when he was 24, but still managed to play saxophone in a local polka band. I suppose you could write a story about that, something sappy about overcoming adversity.

I suppose you could also argue that the dinner these three shared was a conflict — or at least a contradiction — to turkey traditions, for they dined on homemade kielbasa, baked potatoes, canned corn and green beans, dill pickles, bread, and a fancily frosted store-bought cake. No birds, no cranberries, no pumpkin pie. Their oven was a microwave, and they drank Coca-Cola and Squirt, garnished from the bar's stores and served over ice in short, stubby glasses.

They didn't dine at a fancy round or oval table, but at one of eight small square tables in the barroom. Tables stained dark, dark brown, then marked with a slightly lighter cross where hundreds of knuckle-thumping, card-slapping, trick-taking euchre players had worn away the stain. Tables that had been sloshed with spilt beer and wiped down more times than anyone could remember or care to count. They didn't sit in fancy, padded chairs. But simple, straight-back barroom chairs. Functional chairs, akin to those broken over heads in old Western movies.

The barroom decorations were not serene autumn brown and homey pumpkin orange, but blue, red, and white of rah-rah football and brew. An inflatable beach ball, shaped like a helmet with face mask, hung from a hook in the center of the ceiling. Irregular bold type on a Budweiser poster of a super-charged stock car roared, "wE rAce for Beer." A sign above the liquor shelf behind the bar proclaimed, "We don't charge TAX, we collect it."

Martin and Bob were father and son. Lorraine, a younger sister to Martin's first wife, had not seen the two men in years. In early November, knowing things would be different this holiday season, Bob had asked his dad what he wanted to do for Thanksgiving and Martin had replied, "Visit your mother's relatives."

Bob had felt umbilical then as he pictured large turkey dinners from his youth, when aunts and uncles from the 13-sibling Schulte clan ate in one of their small country kitchens crammed with people who joked and laughed amid savory aromas. Back then, he and cousins had scampered through upstairs bedrooms and played hide-and-seek amidst dusty bales of hay and straw in an immense barn. They had breathed cool autumn air sweetened by the smell of cattle and chickens. "Who do you want to visit?" he had asked.

"Let's start with Lorraine and go from there."

"How long do you want to stay?"

"Oh, let's just play it by ear." After a pause, Martin had continued. "Maybe a couple of days, or three."

So, on Thanksgiving day, at mid-morn, the two men had driven north out of Port Huron, where the middle of the five Great Lakes flows into the St. Clair River. Bob had hoped they would take U.S. 25, which ran along the shore, but his father had chosen an inland route, past the Dorsey House and through Croswell, Peck, and Sandusky. Into the part of the state where most surnames are polysyllabic, blessed with more letters than necessary, and end with "sky" or "ski." Lorraine's Bill had been a Lackowski. A Pheasant Tail Contest plaque in his honor rested on a shelf inside a glass trophy case in the barroom. Names engraved on the plaque's brass plates, along with dimensions just slightly shorter or longer than 24 inches, included Gornowich, Alent, Gusa, and, appropriately, Hunt. Of O'Berski, Bob asked, "Is he Irish or Polish?"

"Hard to tell," his aunt replied. "Must be half and half." She spoke carefully and with unusual inflection, the result of an overbite. When you're one of 13, some things don't get fixed.

Lorraine served the first round of drinks at the bar. Like the tables, it was dark brown, except for the raised, ash elbow rail on the customer side. This was worn smooth by forearms covered with farmer flannel and stained with sweat from dusty summer haying — smoother with dirt and time than could be accomplished with fine grit emery. The wooden floor next to the bar sloped a gentle two inches lower than the rest of the room and the bar tilted slightly toward it, the accumulative effect of customers' weight as they, farmers with wind-reddened cheeks and hat-protected white foreheads, stood and jawed about rotten weather and decent yields that produced less and less profit. The floor in the restrooms, labeled Kings and Queens, did the same, with the deepest depression being just in front of the single antiquated urinals and toilets.

"Where are your children today?" Bob asked as they ate. There wasn't much sound in the room, at least not when the overhead heaters kicked off, and they didn't come on again until after their feet were cold.

"Betty's in Utah; her husband wanted to stay there after he was discharged from the Army. Patti is in Saginaw. And the boys are busy. Ron is probably out hunting with Brian." She went on to describe how her grandson had shot his first buck this year, at age 16, after getting glasses. "The doctor was surprised that he had gotten his driver's license, his eyes were so bad," she said. "He had been doing poorly in school, but they didn't know there was a problem until he missed an easy shot on opening day."

After the meal, Bob asked if they wanted to visit anyone else. "Irene is in the hospital," Lorraine replied, and the three drove to visit her sister in Bad Axe.

In the small, three-story hospital, the elders talked — Irene with difficulty because of tubes in her nose. She didn't seem to know that she had fallen and broken her hip. "Strokes," Lorraine explained later. Bob wandered into the solarium looking for a television that would update him on the Lions and Bears. He found a set, but couldn't find an "on" switch. So he ducked into a vacant room, reached high to turn on and tune in the overhead TV, and leaned against a freshly sheeted bed. There, he picked up the score — tied at 20 early in the third quarter — and saw a dropped third down pass and a punt return before Lorraine poked her head in and told him it was time to go. "I don't like hospitals," she said on the way to the elevator.

Another short drive failed to locate brother-in-law Norm Wolschleger at the farm house that Bob had so fondly remembered from his youth. But in the barn, he found remnants of straw in near-empty lofts, a Gehl haylage box standing immovable on four 50-gallon drums, and a few loaves of hardening bread left for the peacock and two peahens that flew from hand-hewn beam to hand-hewn beam. He looked through gaping holes where side planks had fallen away, leaving their weathered neighbors. The wind blew against his face and through his jacket. The skies were gray and darkening. And suddenly he felt a great urge to piss, which he did through a hole in the side of the barn toward the base of a now-empty silo, its staves held in place by rusted girdling rods.

"Anyone else?" he asked upon returning to the car and taking his place behind the wheel.

"There's no one else left," Lorraine replied.

"We could play some cards," Martin suggested.

Back at the Parisville Bar, Lorraine pulled a deck from a cabinet near the end of the bar. "You know how to play euchre, don't you, Bob?" Her eyes twinkled with the tease.

"My parents taught me when I was six," he replied in kind while rubbing his father's slouched shoulders. "But there are only three of us."

"Then shoot the moon. You play that, don't you, Marty?"

"Sure," he said with a vigorous voice.

A hole drilled through the near center of the deck showed that the red-backed cards had once graced the inside of a casino. The solitary pip on the ace of hearts was punctured through the right ventricle.

Conversation flowed through seven games, which Lorraine

scored on two sheets of colored scrap paper. Mostly she talked about her customers, the 23 years that she and Bill had run the place together, and that now, after four years on her own, she wasn't going to renew the liquor license when it expired next April.

"Can you sell the bar?" Martin asked.

"No one buys bars any more."

Bob remembered the two nearby taverns, lonely country establishments amidst flat and fertile farmland, they had passed within a few miles on their earlier jaunt. Two others, Lorraine had said, were closed and converted into some other kind of businesses.

During the fifth game, at half past six, the first customers of the day walked in. An elderly couple and their two young grandsons. They ordered two draft beers, a Coke, and a Payday, and sat on four of the seven red-topped bar stools. The boys swiveled back and forth. The grandparents talked of cards and card tournaments, and the woman said that she had played over 2,400 games so far this year and that she was planning on keeping track again next year. Lorraine told that she had recently played 30 in one day, while also tending bar, and invited the couple to sit in, but they declined.

"How late do you stay open?" Martin asked after the customers left.

"Until there's no one here."

"Doesn't the state regulate a closing time?" Bob asked.

"Five," she bid. "Two-thirty. With the last call at two. But if no one is here, I'll close early. And if I have to run errands during the day, I lock up and go." Her laugh was quick and seasoned. "Some customers don't like that, but I tell them that they can go to the dentist for me." She paused. "And I can't open before seven. What are you going to do?" She looked at Bob, who sat on her left.

"Pass," he replied.

"Pass," said Martin.

"Spades." She led with the right bower, lightly rapping her knuckles square in the center of the table.

"I wonder what she would have done if we hadn't been there today," Bob said to his dad on their way back to Port Huron that night. They were on U.S. 25. On their left, the blackness of Lake Huron was marred only by lights from two freighters in the shipping channel five miles out.

Martin stared down the road, watching icy rain accumulate before being swept away by intermittent wipers.

Black of the Moonless Night

Wind blew and rain poured and people dreamed what the Riders wanted them to dream. Dreams implanted in restless sleep to mask the stallions' howl. The howl of their hooves, the howl of their nostrils, the howl of their fury — loud and constant and fierce. Unlike any howl known in the land, a howl that raged only in blackest night. And into that blackest night, the Riders rode, sending their thoughts ahead of them. Thoughts of the sky, clear and blue and high. A beautiful day. A perfect day.

But even through countless journeys over countless centuries, the Riders had never seen blue skies. Their thoughts of sunshine came from their victims, people of the daytime who confessed of making love during golden dawns and under crimson sunsets. Victims who shuddered with the telling and hurt with the knowing they would never love again.

As they rode, the Riders dared not think of their Master, but they also could not remove Him from their minds for He forced them to think of Him. And His image maddened the palettes they projected. So in the people's dreams, the sky was not quite blue, the colors not quite true, the hues not quite complete. White cirrus clouds contained a hint of red lascivious lips. Then the people also dreamed that that cannot be.

Except in dreams. Dreams they shared as they lay curled in their sleeping bags and under blankets and in the streets. They did not know that they — all of them, the adventurous cocooned in their down, the rich wrapped in satin, and the poor covered by cardboard — shared the same dream. If asked while sanely awake, they would tell each other that dreams are unique. But on this night of the insane, it was not so.

The people sensed this only when the Riders were close and the dreams so intense that shrieks and screams arose. First from babies and little ones and the old and feeble and innocents with pure minds, then the others, too. They all screamed, and their screams echoed back to the Riders, and the Riders knew they were near. Their victims were near.

The screams were so loud that the people heard only screams and ignored the wind and did not notice the rain and did not remember the Demon in their dreams and did not hear the Riders. The people stood with their mouths agape and eyes dazed and knew, too late, that it was too late.

The Riders — an evil storm on an evil night on an evil mission — swept them away, leaving a vacuum silence — eerie and calm — and fertile soil for the seed, the next crop to be sown. The next generation of blood and flesh and malleable minds to be fattened then plundered by the Riders when they come again, in the black of the moonless night.

Full Moon Gathering

Carol took a caribou hide from her van, and we joined the ring of people seated around the fire. I removed my TopSiders and felt the caribou's fur with my feet. It was incredibly soft, and my mind resurrected an old Native American saying, "He who wears only moccasins knows a world made only of leather." The thought startled me. I had heard it many years earlier in a previous life of wing tips, button-down collars, power ties, three-piece blues, and formal business presentations. I had chuckled at the idiocy of the statement then and dismissed it. Why did I think of it now? "Why analyze?" Carol would have said if she could read my thoughts. I looked at her and saw her looking at me. She squeezed my hand and nodded.

A college-age blonde with hair that fell to her waist sat in a lotus position and sang about Mother Earth. "Oh, Mama. Oooh, Mama. I feel you beneath my feet ... ." She carried the lilting lyric as Full Mooners beat on tom-toms, congas, and drums of varied shapes and sizes. Even a long shipping tube with one plastic end still attached. How ironic, I thought, from whose loading dock did you originate?

I looked around the ring. Clothing punctuated eclecticism — old-west denim, Banana Republic khaki, and bright Bahaman Ts. Light-weight, colorful long skirts that brought back images of the '60s. A young boy with high-top tennis shoes and red flashing lights in the soles. The group's leader had black pants and shoes, punctuated by green socks. Women outnumbered bras.

I closed my eyes and music poured into my ears. Soft soprano lyrics weaved through loud bass drumming and staccatoing sticks. My body swayed. I felt caribou at my feet and massaged it with toes and fingers. The fire warmed me. Smoke wafted into my nose. Visible words flowed from voices. Notes fluttered like gypsy moths on treble clef staffs of gray smoke. Could I see the beat? Was it definitive, qualitative, quantitative? No, black bass crickets hopped randomly in dewy green grass. But then two or three hopped in unison, then more, picking up the beat. Soon, cadence had harmony and all crickets hopped as one. Everyone drummed together.

Carol placed her hand on my leg. Listen again, more closely, she seemed to tell me. Feel rhythm with your heart. Everyone is not quite together. Some drums pronounce bass, a driving force — thump, thump, thump — like emerging links. Above that surface sound, other drums beat harmonic. Syncopation accents bass as some of the deepest drums offer extra strokes — da-da, thump, thump — that both match and mismatch.

Carol guided my hand to the top of her drum, a bodhran. Clasping my hand in hers, she placed my fingertips gently on the drumhead and I felt group force, vibrations that came from all with no distinction of origin, size, nor drummers' strengths. Visual adjectives — old, young, heavy, slender, tanned, long-haired, black and white and green — became trivial.

"Individuality amidst unity." I was surprised at the sound of my voice. I opened my eyes and looked around to see if anyone had heard, to see if anyone was watching me. No one was, except Carol, and she was smiling. Her knowing eyes seemed to probe my mind and confirm the message.

She offered me the bodhran. I took it, but didn't beat it. I let my fingertips linger on its head, feeling, receiving, absorbing percussion from other drums that rained upon me through the instrument in my hands. This was all the confirmation I needed.

After we stopped drumming, a young man read a poem about synergy, about need and desire for others. I wanted to mention my discovery, the discovery to which Carol had led me. Should I? I'm new here. Would I be repeating what they already understand?

No one spoke. The young man looked at each person ringing the fire. I followed his eyes and studied their faces, too. "There's synergy in the drumming," I said finally. "If you stop and place your fingertips on the drumhead, you'll feel the vibrations of others. Synergy flows among all of us." Carol slid her arm around my lower back, and I turned to smile at her. "We give energy to others as we simultaneously receive it."

"Giving is the same as receiving."

I looked at the young man in amazement as his words hung over the fire. It's that simple, isn't it?

In the closing moments of the gathering, we stood in a circle holding hands, the full moon rising through towering pines. A man beside me said, "Thank you for what you said. I had never experienced that before."

I smiled at him. There is so much I have not yet experienced.

Unexpected

Leaves had not yet spent
their arboreous hold

And jack-o-lanterns had not yet graced
their terrible night

When snow and ice came driven
by ferocious wind

To wrench fiber from fiber
in crashing cascade

And bring to the ground
communities of leaves

And humble their hosts
with deformities untold

Like lovers who leave their scars
exposed to the cold.

Age 12

Eight weeks after brain surgery, his lady friend, April, told him he was 12. That was progress.

Only six weeks earlier, he had been an infant blessed with euphoria and possessed by depression. And the switch was often flipped without warning. There had been one night when he had laughed and talked with April on the phone, then misconstrued an innocent remark and spewed vinegar and venom at her. He had curled his body, tucked his knees under his chin, and cried uncontrollable infant tears. Then, he was ashamed and held the telephone behind his back as far from his face as he could reach. He thought about hanging up, but he could hear her voice calling his name, and the need for connection prevailed. He clutched the phone with both panic and realization that it was his life line.

Ten days later, he had experienced the "terrible two's." It was a gorgeous Sunday afternoon, and there was no logical reason to throw a temper tantrum, but he had. He had lain on his tummy on the floor, kicked his feet and pounded his fists. His 18-year-old daughter watched as her "parent" stretched his hand to her. Through blinding tears, he said something about the Neil Diamond song, "Brother Love's Traveling Salvation Show," about reaching out your hand to help others and reaching out the other hand to God. Still, his hand hung in mid-air as his daughter refused to extend her hand to him. Instead, she watched him as though he were a creature in the zoo. Not a known creature like an alligator or a tiger, but some new anomaly, a cross between the body of a mature man and the emotions of an infant. She had watched from a safe distance, afraid of being pulled into whatever was happening to him. He cried and exclaimed words he immediately chose to forget.

Two days later, he "ran away" and had done it "all by myself" even though his daughter had taken him to the Amtrak station and his dad had picked him up at the other end of the line. In his mind, he was five.

Age 12 came after a night of dancing. While cooking a late-night stir fry, April commented on friends at the club. She said the youngest couple was the loudest and most vocal. The oldest couple said little, but their comments contained the greatest wisdom and demeanor.

He asked April where they, being of an age in the middle, fit into the spectrum. "In the middle," she said, "but you say a few things that draw attention to yourself."

"What do you mean?" he asked.

"Well, several times you said to me, 'Thank you for being here.' And I think you say it just to draw attention to yourself."

The roof fell. Glass shattered. He imploded. "We don't see enough of each other," he shouted as he paced the room, fists clenched. "I love your company. I was happy to be with you, and my 'thank yous' were genuine, earnest remarks." His voiced cracked with tears, and he turned away from her, looking through the glass patio door that both reflected his image and showed the blackness of the night.

"Hon, I wanted to be with you. You don't have to thank me for that."

He turned. "Oh, but I do have to thank you, April. You could have chosen to be somewhere else, with someone else. You chose to be with me. That is worthy of 'thank you.'"

He turned from the patio door and stomped through the dining room and into the kitchen. He leaned against the refrigerator, his shoulders rounded, his head hanging in front of him. His feet extended slightly, his posture bad. He could have been in a junior high hallway leaning against a locker.

April came to him. They hugged. Uncle Ben's rice simmered on the stove. Neither of them had set a timer or looked at the clock.

"You don't have to thank me when we're together," she said.

He pushed her back a bent-arm's length and cited instances when he had begged for her companionship and she had refused. "Less than two weeks after surgery, I called on a Saturday night and asked you to tune to a certain radio station that was playing good dance music. You didn't. I wanted to make a connection over the air waves, and you wouldn't do it."

"But — "

"And there were other times, too," he sobbed. "April, I had to beg. You wanted to break up last spring. You had said that you were going to visit me in the hospital and that would be 'it' between us. I felt you pulling away. So, when you decide to be with me for an evening of dancing, I think that is worthy of a 'thank you.'"

He walked to the counter and began to cut a squash. His knife cut through each slice with a resounding clack on the cutting board. "And I will continue to say 'thank you' for our time together because our time together is special to me. Very special. And if you have a problem with that, that is your business. But I am darn glad to be with you every time we are together. And if I feel like telling you that, I will." Clack. Clack.

April gently took the knife from his hand and finished cutting the squash. He slouched in a chair. "You don't understand me," he said. "You don't understand what I have been going through. And I have been going through it alone. And I don't like that. So being with you is very darn special to me."

She started to pour the veggies into the skillet. He came to the stove and helped her. They hugged again. Several times, he repeated that she didn't understand him and that being together was special. She held him and listened.

After a long moment, he took three steps back from her and said, "Last night, we talked about how I look like a man, but I feel like a toddler. Since I look like a man, people expect me to think and act like a man. But my thoughts are confused. I am rebuilding my memory and my reasoning just like a toddler learns new things. I am relearning some things that I know I have learned in the past, but those memories are gone, and I have to rebuild them."

He waved one hand above his head. "You are at this level, April. You think of work and budgets and your house." He waved his other hand horizontally below his belt. "I am down here. My basic needs are to be held and hugged and loved. As an adult, I have to be responsible for my finances, my daughter, my house, my business, my clients, my relationship with you. I know I have to do that, but my basic need is to be hugged."

She looked at him, and he knew she did not understand. He had learned to recognize that look in people's eyes. No one could understand the dichotomy of his external adult and his internal child. People say they understand, but they don't.

He had also learned to accept that, but he really wanted April to understand, so he stepped toward her and hugged her again, his hands tense around her waist, his back hunched, his chin behind her shoulder. "April, don't try to think of the toddler in me. Rather, think of your children when they were very young. What did they act like when they were growing up? Think of them, and maybe you will understand me."

He felt April's tears change.

"You're not a toddler," she sobbed. "You're 12. You're just like my Scott when he left home to live with his dad. He acted just like you, and there wasn't anything I could do to help him, either." And she wept from deep within.

He changed, too; his "child" went away and his "adult" emerged. He stood taller so that April's head could rest on his shoulder. His hands moved higher on her back, one stroked her hair. He thought, but did not say, there, there; it will be all right.

The stir fry sizzled.

He was 12.

The First Thing I'm Gonna Do

"Dad," Mandie, my six-year-old, said as I turned my car onto our street, "the first thing I'm gonna do when we get home is go to the bathroom."

"The first thing?" I asked.

"The very first thing," she replied.

"Do you think you should go into the bathroom and close the door first?"

"Well, yes." She hesitated for a moment. "And I guess I should pull down my jeans, too."

"That would save a mess," I quipped, and she giggled with slight embarrassment. "And I think you'll need to walk through the house and climb the stairs before you go into the bathroom."

She came back quickly, "I'll have to go through the front door before doing that."

"Go through the door?" I teased. "Please unlock and open it first, unless you've become Casper."

She laughed, "Oh, Dad."

"And I hope you'll get out of the car and walk to the house before going into the house," I continued.

"I'll even wait for the car to stop," she said with a playful pout.

"Good," I complimented her as I pulled into our driveway.

"Dad," she said, sparkling with charm, "the first thing I'm gonna do when we get home is watch you stop the car, then I'm gonna unbuckle my seat belt, and give you a big hug."

"Then what are you going to do?"

"Go to the bathroom."

Oh, Gluttonous Christmas Tree

Oh, gluttonous. Oh, gluttonous,
Oh, gluttonous Christmas Tree.

Made of fakey plastic green,
Site of hideous Yuletide scene.

Towering a full ten feet tall
Makes even grownups feel empty and small.

It consumes eight strands of holiday lights,
Blue, red, yellow and orangish bright.

Twinkly snowflakes descend in electric cascade
Amidst three dozen toy lanterns in Singapore made.

Ornaments abound under garland and greed
Laden with more than any tree needs.

For the ornaments are large and small
Some farfetched, ridiculous all:

Trains, wagons, trucks, and two-seater bikes,
Dogs, cats, monkeys, and bears on trikes.

Scarlett O'Hara next to fire truck fumes,
Fiddles, Holly Fairy, and peacock plumes.

Mickey, Minnie, Donald, and Pluto
grate off-key carols from loud clocks o' cuckoo.

And four white angels, six-inches round
contrast two stuffed Santas weighing each a pound.

The tree is topped with a night-shirted bear
Perched with open arms as if to share.

For the presents come glitzy and galore,
And the tree welcomes them: more, more, more.

Until they are piled higher than a bib,
Hiding Mary and Joseph and Christ in his crib.

While children outside, hungry and cold
Curse Christmas with silent fury untold.

And the homeless at the mission
would welcome the money spent on one ceramic kitten.

Strawberries
(an essay)

A few years ago during a time of quiet reflection, I made a simple discovery. I was picking strawberries with friends who were intent on harvesting a case or two each. I, on the other hand, wanted only a couple of quarts. While they picked, I enjoyed the cool evening at sunset, listened to their conversation wafting across the windless field, and unconsciously nibbled a strawberry.

Then I realized that little bit tasted just as good as if I had consumed the entire berry in one bite. I took another small nibble, rolling it across my tongue, savoring its essence. Then I took another small nibble. Then another. And another. Maybe a dozen nibbles in all to eat just *one* berry. Later, I did the same with a piece of strawberry pie. A little bit tasted just as good as a lot. Each bite extended the deliciousness.

Over the next few days, I tried this controlled consumption on everything from grapes to steaks. Even peas, raisins, nuts, and M&Ms can be eaten one at a time rather than by the handful.

Which brings me to the way in which we've been consuming land, especially farmland, wetlands, green spaces, and natural animal habitat. Why does our human species think we need cathedral homes, often inhabited by only two people, that are larger than farm houses in which a family of a dozen dwelled a few decades ago? Why do we think we need new stores when we have vacant shops and dwindling downtowns? Why do we think we need an abundance of impervious concrete when indigenous grass, wildflowers, trees, and shrubs are more beautiful and beneficial? Why do we think we need to travel afar, consuming petroleum resources along the way, when we have so much natural scenery nearby, often within biking distances?

I think the answer is because we've become accustomed to stuffing our cheeks with strawberries. We're being told and taught to clutter our walls and closets and drawers, and to fill our land and landfills with the blight of materialistic gluttony.

Consider the visual images that television commercials feed us: the man who gobbles an entire piece of pizza; four young singers who each guzzle an entire can of pop; consumer channels that would have us buy, buy, buy without leaving our homes rather than look around and appreciate what we already own.

Before learning to walk and talk, children are being taught that the one with the most toys wins. Instant telecommunication is stuffing adult minds with a false urgency to be everywhere at once.

We're being told to grab the newest, biggest, brightest, fastest, and best without regard for what we already are responsible, and certainly without regard for proper disposal of what we no longer need or want once we have the *next* newest, biggest, brightest, fastest, and best.

Fortunately, there are other messages also being spoken: to unclutter our homes and live more simply, more creatively, and more productively; to reuse vacated land and preserve open spaces.

In short, as I learned a few years ago, we need not gobble in order to enjoy. Rather, let's savor the places where we literally and figuratively plant and pick fruit, places inside and outside our homes where we peacefully taste, a little bit at a time, the natural joys of life.

About the Author

Bob Weir is a freelance writer and communications consultant. He writes contract assignments for governmental, organizational, and corporate clients and magazine articles about people, outdoor adventures, and environmental issues.

His articles have appeared in Encore, Maritime Life and Traditions, Michigan Out-of-Doors, Multihulls, and Sail magazines and the Port Huron Times Herald newspaper.

Notable projects include development of customized management training curricula and writing a 20-page tabloid on water quality and quantity in Michigan for Detroit Newspapers in Education, the St. Clair County Master Recreation Plan, and the St. Clair County Master Plan for land use, which the Michigan Society of Planners rewarded as "the best-written, most-readable" master plan in Michigan in 2000.

A native of Emmett, Mich., Bob currently lives in Port Huron with his wife and father, but also claims Kalamazoo as a home. His daughter Mandie lives in Georgia. In addition to writing, Bob likes to dance, sail, backpack, bicycle, and participate in other outdoor silent sports, be involved with environmental protection and preservation, and give and receive massage.